Joe Murphy was born in 1979 in Enniscorthy, County Wexford where he lived for nineteen years before dying. Then he got better.

He was educated in Enniscorthy VEC, from where he went on to study English in University College Dublin. After undertaking a Masters in Early Modern Drama, he went on to qualify as a secondary school teacher. He has had poetry published in an anthology of Enniscorthy writers, and his first novel, *1798: Tomorrow The Barrow We'll Cross*, was published in 2011 by Liberties Press. His job is teaching.

You wouldn't believe the stories.

First published in 2012 by
Liberties Press
7 Rathfarnham Road | Terenure | Dublin 6W
Tel: +353 (1) 405 5701
www.libertiespress.com | info@libertiespress.com

Trade enquiries to Gill & Macmillan Distribution
Hume Avenue | Park West | Dublin 12
T: +353 (1) 500 9534 | F: +353 (1) 500 9595 | E: sales@gillmacmillan.ie

Distributed in the UK by
Turnaround Publisher Services
Unit 3 | Olympia Trading Estate | Coburg Road | London N22 6TZ
T: +44 (0) 20 8829 3000 | E: orders@turnaround-uk.com

Distributed in the United States by
Dufour Editions | PO Box 7 | Chester Springs | Pennsylvania 19425

ISBN: 978-1-907593-45-1
2 4 6 8 10 9 7 5 3 1

A CIP record for this title is available from the British Library.

Cover design by Fidelma Slattery
Internal design by Liberties Press
Printed by Bell & Bain Ltd

The publishers gratefully acknowledge
financial assistance from the Arts Council.

Dead Dogs

Joe Murphy

The red stuff that Seán's lying in definitely isn't blood. It's too red red. It's not warm enough and it's not dark enough and it's not like the stuff coming from his nose.

For Seán, the world must rock to the concussion of being blind-sided.

Today I've lost the best part of my life.

This is the day, with the sun rabies-hot in the sky and every face in the Market Square hanging open. Every mouth is a shocked black hole and I don't know what I'm screaming but I'm screaming something.

How we, how me and Seán, get here, takes some explaining.

Seán is not a well person. He never has been. We are sixteen years of age and for as long as I've known him, Seán has not been like the rest of us. Seán is big. Way bigger than me. He has these massive hands and a dead splat starfish of blonde hair squashed onto his head. In hurling he'd make a great fullback. If he played hurling. Instead Seán does stuff to things. To birds and cats and dogs. He does *stuff* to them.

Seán is not well.

In spite of this, Seán is my best friend. We grew up, I suppose we're still growing up, outside town on the road out to the Still. For years I lived out there with Seán until me and my Da had to move back into town. The road is narrow and windy and there are ditches and trees and fields swarming up close to it on both sides. When we were young, there wasn't a lot of people living out our way. Just a necklace of bungalows and detached dormers. This is what my geography teacher calls *ribbon*, or *linear*, *development*. In the fields now there are fungus growths of half-finished estates chewing gummily at the sky. In their scaffolding the hard accents of Eastern Europe used to rattle amongst the ironwork. They're all quiet now. This is what our geography teacher calls *urban sprawl*. This is what she calls *economic migration*. This is what our history teacher calls the legacy of the Building Boom. The aborted twin of the Celtic Tiger. Something misshapen and bawling and coated in concrete dust.

These new estates, they crawl up out of the muck and they slump and spill across our childhood. The field we built our fort in is gone now under a bristle of empty semi-detached houses. *Fairglade*, they called it. Seán wants to know what's so fucking fair about it.

For years me and Seán had the run of the fields all to

ourselves. For years me and Seán were the only two boys on our road. It's funny, but even now I'm thinking of it as *our* road. Even when all the others started arriving it was still *our* road. The others with their new cars and accents that came from somewhere between Greystones and Pearse Station. Accents that started a million miles from Killann or Monart. A million miles from where they were born.

In a hundred years everyone in Ireland will speak like they're from the Mid-Atlantic. Everyone will sound like a DJ.

The people arrived on our road and mostly what they brought with them was money and new cars. But sometimes what they brought with them was other children. Now these children were more like me than Seán. This wasn't hard.

Seán, when he was little, didn't like this. Seán, when he was little, knew he wasn't like the others. Knew he wasn't like me.

The sun's a spangle of tinsel through tree branches and the football hops across the lawn. Me and the lads are kicking and scrapping for any sort of a touch. Jumpers for goalposts. Everyone's a hectic milling of arms and legs and everyone's a bundle of laughter. Everyone except Seán. Seán's just standing there. And he's not standing off to one side either. He's standing in the middle of the lawn and he's turning as we play around him. Turning with his round eyes flat as stones. Turning with this weird half-smile on his face. His mouth is a shallow, liver-coloured curve and he's turning, turning, alone in the middle of all our games.

He does this a lot.

Alone in the middle of our games, he stands there and watches all of us lads who are different from him. We all know what's going to happen next but no one wants to stop playing. To stop our manic football would mean we had to recognise Seán's difference. And if we recognised it, we'd have to do something about it. So we ignore him and every minute that goes by is one minute closer to what's going to happen.

Then Seán's moving and now he's grabbing the ball and now he's running away with it. When you're five or six this is just an excuse to chase somebody, you don't see anything shifting underneath. You don't care why you're running. You don't care that some of the boys, some of the older boys, don't think this is funny anymore.

One thing that always stands out like a wart in my memory is that Seán would only ever give the ball back to me. No matter who owned it, he would never, ever, give it back to them. Not ever. Not even when next summer the lads start to beat him. Not even when next summer with tears in his eyes and blood climbing the cracks between his teeth and he has to hide in the coal shed, would he give them back the ball.

Ever since that day, I have to get the ball back on my own. The lads make me because the sound of Seán's big fist breaking Jamie Anderson's nose, I think, makes everyone afraid. Not me though. I've never been afraid of Seán. Not even when the bad things start to happen.

But that was then and this is now.

Now Seán has to take these little red tablets that sort of glisten like they're moist. They're the same colour as Mrs Kehoe's lips. She's the school's Home School Liaison Officer and she's the one who first says that something has to change with Seán. She's the one who first says that *drastic measures* have to be taken.

Seán's not great at English, so when he asks me what this means, I tell him it means he's fucked.

This is a couple of months ago now but Dr Thorpe arrives at Seán's house and I'm watching him get out of his big black 407 and I'm watching him watching the car as the central locking beeps and the lights flash. In his hand, he has a black, leather, Jack-the-Ripper doctor's case. It looks bulbous and pregnant. Dr Thorpe looks like what Pat Kenny would look like if he found a sense of humour somewhere. He has perfectly coiffeured hair that has the gossamer glimmer of too much hair spray. How much is too much? When he smiles, his whole face shines and the muscles covering his skull contract and his talk-show host's hair lifts in a solid, chemically bonded mass. I always thought it was weird the way he smiled and he sees me watching him and now he's smiling this smile and now he's waving at me with his car keys still bunched in his fist.

After what happened with my Mam, I'm not sure I like Dr Thorpe. Because of this, I just stand there without waving back until a JCB comes yellow and rumbling up the road and when it's gone so is Dr Thorpe. I don't know why he's gone into Seán's house but I'm thinking it must have something to do with what Mrs Kehoe said.

The next time I see Seán we're in school and he's showing me these lipstick-red tablets he has to take twice a day after food. He shakes the white tub they come in and you can hear the brittle rattle of each individual tablet. Each individual *drastic measure*.

The tablets aren't very big so they're easy to swallow and Seán doesn't think they could contain much of anything. I'm smiling and then I'm punching him in the shoulder. I tell him he doesn't need much. That there's nothing wrong with him. But I know that he knows I'm lying.

I don't know what's in the tablets and Seán doesn't want to show them to Mr Connolly. Mr Connolly's sound and teaches science and I'm pretty confident he'll know what they are. Seán doesn't want anyone to know though. It's like he's embarrassed, and when these three girls come along the corridor where we're sitting, he shoves the tub deep deep into his pocket. I just look at him for a moment as the girls titter and lean together and froth about something we probably couldn't give two fucks about. Then they're gone and Seán, not looking at me, shakes his head and says, 'I'm such a freak.'

My first memory of Seán comes from so way long ago that I don't even know what age we were. All I know is we were old enough to be eating Tayto. And I remember the heat. The delicious, honeyed heat of summer. I'm sitting on a wall and that deluge of warmth is emptying out of an open sky and soaking into the back of my neck and drenching through the fabric of my T-shirt. I'm licking my lips and they feel tacky with the drying syrup of Dunnes Stores cola. It must be a birthday party or something because my pudgy little boy's hands are sticky too and their gummy bundles of fingers are clutching a bag of cheese and onion Tayto. I'm not sure if the bags have gotten smaller over the years or whether it's just that time is a magnifying glass but I'm sure this one was as big as I was.

I'm sitting, baking, on this little concrete wall and my sugar-sticky digits are making popping noises against the plastic of the Tayto packet. I'm sitting, baking, on this little concrete wall and my mouth is watering and now I'm hearing a voice behind me. It's going, 'Don't open them like that.'

I'm turning around on the wall now and as I change position the hot concrete is almost painful where it touches my legs below the cuffs of my shorts. My legs are maggot white. I remember that. They are the colour of fish bellies.

Behind me there's this thick, tree-stump of a boy. He's tall but his width makes him look stocky and below his blond Beatles' fringe these weird flat eyes blink at me once and refocus with the calm deliberation of an owl. And now this thick, tree-stump of a boy, he's shaking his head and going, 'You can't open them like that.'

I remember I'm staring at him and then I'm looking at my mauled and crinkled bag of crisps and then I'm looking at him again. To those weird, vacant eyes I must look like one of those nodding dogs in the back window of a car.

I go, 'Why not?'

The other boy's wearing dungarees and they scrape and rasp as he's climbing up onto the wall beside me. His eyes meet mine, then look away, meet mine, then look away and his big right hand points to the packet of Tayto. His fingers are covered with an ooz-ing darkness like he's been eating chocolate spread with his fists. His big right hand points to the packet of Tayto and he's saying, 'You can't open Tayto on the red side.'

In my hand the Tayto bag is banded red at the top and blue at the bottom. I'm looking at the picture of Mr Spud on the front and he seems to be opening his packet on the red side. I point this out to the other boy, 'The Tayto man's opening his like I do.'

'Yeah, but you're not supposed to.'

The big blond boy won't look at me properly and the way he keeps snatching glances before staring at the ground again is starting to creep me out.

I was always a petulent child, I probably still am, and just to show him I can do what I want with my own Tayto, my small pink crabs of hands crawl up the packet and curl about its red top. They curl about its red top and now they're pulling and now they're stopping because the boy beside me is starting to moan. I'm surprised by this and now I'm going, 'What's wrong? Are you okay?'

The boy stops moaning and puts his face in his hands. From between his fingers his voice sounds distorted and a long way off, 'If you open the red side bad things might come.'

Here is the moment to bear in mind that I don't know how old I am but it's so long ago that I can't remember. I'm so young that the blond boy's words scare the life out of me and I'm suddenly saying, 'Okay. Okay. I'll open them the other way round.'

These words of mine, they come out in a wet rush the way later that evening I'll sick up all the sweets and all the Tayto and all the Dunnes Stores cola.

The boy lifts his face out of his hands and watches silently as I upend the Tayto and tug open the blue-banded bottom of the packet. Looking inside I can see the golden flakes of deep-fried potato all shattered into savoury slivers. Beside me, the blond boy is looking at them as well and his thick lips wriggle wide across his face and split into a grin.

'Thank you,' he says. 'I'm Seán Galvin.'

'That's alright,' I say. 'Want a Tayto?'

From that day to this, Seán, when he sees anyone opening a packet of Tayto on the red side, he has to either cover his face so he can't see or he tells them to turn it upside down. I don't know why he does this but Seán and me spent most of Baby Infants convincing people to eat their Tayto from the blue side. Anyone who went to school for any length of time with Seán Galvin, give them a packet of Tayto and straightaway they'll turn it upside down. Mr Connolly says this is *Pavlovian Conditioning*. Mr Connolly says this has nothing to do with the dessert.

A lot of people think Seán is strange. Including me. Seán isn't like any of the rest of us. I don't believe that bad things will happen if you open your Tayto on the wrong side but even when Seán isn't around I still open them the way he'd want me to. This is the effect Seán has. A lot of people are frightened of Seán. Not me though. When bad things finally start to happen, Seán says he didn't mean to. That he can't remember. But I know he can. There's a light in Seán's eyes sometimes. There and gone like a will-o'-the-wisp. I know the bad things hurt him somewhere inside and I know he's trying to stop. Trying hard. Wormveined and sweating.

I just don't think the tablets will help.

For a start, I'm not sure his Da can afford them. Seán's Mam left him and his Da when Seán was ten. No one knows where she went but my Da says how it was funny that Buckley the milkman shagged off at the same time. Yeah, that's right. The milkman. Our town is a cartoon.

Seán's Da works round the clock but dealing with Seán takes up a lot of his time. He had to sell his car when Seán started his tablets and now he drops him to school in a 1990 Fiesta. Seán doesn't really notice any of this but what he does notice is the fact that men have started to call to his house and argue with his father when they think that Seán's asleep. Seán says he thinks they're foreign but we've kept quiet about this because people like Mags from next door would run down the road screaming about drugs and the Russian Mafia.

Whatever it is, ever since Seán was put on those tablets, his Da seems to be dying a bad death. His jaws are after sinking in and the skin of his face is all tented up over the bones underneath. Every inch of him is after turning the same jaundiced shade as a forty-a-day man's fingers. His whole being is a smoky yellow. I don't want to say it, but coping with Seán is killing him.

Like I said, I don't think the tablets will help.

Another reason I don't think the tablets will help is because I don't think they're doing what they're supposed to be doing. I'm no expert but I'm guessing Seán was put on them because he did things to animals and because some people were scared of him. I'm no expert but I'm guessing the tablets are something like that *Ritalin* stuff that Stephen Pepper in Second Year has to take. Mr Cowper, the Guidance Counsellor, is forever trying to get him off the stuff. Mr Cowper says the school, his parents and society are all *abdicating responsibility*.

I looked it up and what *Ritalin* does is it alters *biochemical pathways*. These pathways are involved in the *screening out* of all the stuff you don't really need to be worried about. Hear that clock ticking? See how it's distracting you? Well *Ritalin* ups the levels of *catecholamines* while, at the same time, it increases your *heart rate*, *blood pressure* and *body temperature* so that you're more alert and you concentrate better. *Ritalin* basically stops you focusing on *irrelevancies* and simultaneaously *suppresses hunger and fatigue*.

What this doesn't tell you is that the spark that lives in people goes out when they take this stuff. I used to play football with Stephen Pepper and now he doesn't play anything. He's just sad all the time.

You take a messed-up teenager, convince them they have a disease and then medicate them until their personality changes to fit your world. The teenager you're left with isn't the teenager you started out with. Instead of discipline you get chemical lobotomies and instead of children you get automotons.

This is the reason I don't think the tablets are working. Seán hasn't changed. He's stopped doing things. He's stopped acting when whatever wrongly wired fuse he has sparks; but I don't think it has anything to do with the tablets. Deep down he hasn't changed. Not at all.

We're sitting in the yard this one day a while ago and Daniel O'Hara's five-year-old brother comes in. It's lunch time and he must have come in to show his big brother the labrador pup that's gambolling ahead of him at the end of its leash. The lolloping puppy is followed by its lolloping master and Mrs O'Hara stands at the school gates, smiling.

Within seconds, everyone's around this puppy like they've never seen anything like it. Some of the Sixth Years amble across, cast their jaded eyes over the scene and then amble off again. If it's not a porn mag they're not interested. The rest of us are, though, and hands are reaching out to stroke, to pet, to ruffle the pup's ears. And, in all this, nobody notices that Seán just stands there. Watching.

Daniel O'Hara arrives. His little frame is charged with indignation and his delicate head is creased pugnaciously around a frown. He's trying to push everyone out of the way and he's roaring, 'Get the fuck away from my dog, ya pack of spas!'

At the sound of his voice the puppy quails. It's velvet head droops and a moment later our group gives way. Daniel's grinning. He's grinning because he obviously hasn't seen his Ma bearing down on him like a storm front. She is the blackest thunderhead on the darkest night and she's spitting lightning.

'Daniel O'Hara! How dare you use language like that in front of your little brother!'

Then she's grabbing him by the ear and thumping him in the back and then Daniel starts to cry.

We spill away, laughing. And I know that Daniel knows nobody will ever, ever, forget this. For the last two years of his school life, Daniel O'Hara will never be able to tell a joke or jeer or take pleasure at someone else's expense. The ring of boys and girls gathered around that puppy will be a noose he'll never, ever, be able to shake off.

And, laughing, I turn to find Seán and, laughing, I turn again.

There's Daniel and his mother. There's his brother, looking confused and in shock at his warring family. So where's Seán? And where's the puppy? Where the *fuck* is the puppy?

And now, not laughing, I turn to run.

I know Seán couldn't have brought the puppy into the school so now I'm running around to the side of it. There's a bristling evergreen hedge at the side but there's a narrow pathway between it and the sports hall. The pathway opens out onto the back of the school and this horrible warren of prefabs that we have to spend half our time in. The prefabs are like ovens in the summer because most of the windows only open four inches before getting stuck, and they're like freezers in the winter because when the windows get stuck you can't unstick them. Every day we sit in these makeshift classrooms with bellying ceilings and watch hundreds of empty four-bedroom semis rear above the trees across the hurling pitch.

I've never run towards the prefabs in my life.

But I'm running towards them now. Towards this plywood ghetto. And I'm thinking, please don't do anything, Seán. I'm running towards this plywood ghetto and I'm hoping to God that the puppy's still alive.

Then I stop. There are ten or twelve prefabs at the back of the school and round here there's not much noise. From over the roof of the sports hall tumble shouts and yells and screams. But here, between the industrial grey of the prefab walls, there's nothing. Not even birdsong.

And now I'm running again, shouting, 'Seán! Where are you?'

Now I'm running right, running left and now I'm running slap bang into Seán.

He's sitting quiet and serene and on his face there's the blank look of the hypnotised. He's sitting quiet and serene on the metal steps of a prefab and the puppy is a limp draping of beige across his lap.

Before I know that I'm saying them, words are hissing from my mouth like blood from an artery, 'My God, Seán, what have you done?'

And like I've said its name, the boneless rag on Seán's lap raises its head and looks at me. The dog is doing this and then Seán is doing this. The two of them silent, doleful. The two of them empty-eyed as addicts.

Then Seán's going, 'What do you think I've done?'

I'm standing here in the muddy heart of a fibreboard slump and I'm suddenly feeling guilty.

And then Seán says something. He says, 'I wanted to. I still want to. He's so soft. You better take him.'

My whole body feels lax and eviscerated.

Numbly I take the puppy and numbly I stroke its head and numbly I watch Seán start to cry.

This is why I don't think the tablets are helping.

What I do think is that Seán can't keep this up. I don't know how he's stopping himself doing stuff like hurting the O'Haras' puppy. I don't know what it's costing him but I think something's going to break.

I'm thinking he *can't* keep this up.

The more I think about it the more I realise that it's not just that Seán doesn't *act* like the rest of us; Seán doesn't *think* like the rest of us either. This is why so many people don't like him. He doesn't understand them and people don't like being misunderstood. He just doesn't get them. Trouble is, nobody gets Seán either.

The more I think about it, the sorrier I feel.

We, Seán and me, are ten years old and we're sitting in this big tree that used to grow three fields down. We are ten years old and we are playing army. When you play army, what you do is you split everyone into two groups and then each group finds a camp and then each group tries to kill the other.

Not literally *kill*.

What you do is, you get all the toy guns, all the hurls, all the bits of sticks you can find and then you use them to shoot with. Everything usually goes fine until one side tries to invade the other's camp. Then people who've been deadly accurate from a field away suddenly start pulling triggers to be met with cries of, 'Ya missed me!'

When this happens, the whole game falls apart and if Nicky Sullivan is playing he'll start to cry. This is because Nicky Sullivan is a quare bad loser. When this happens, everyone will start slagging him and then someone will suggest going down to the pond and our little war will suddenly be forgotten.

The reason that me and Seán are up in this big tree is because we're snipers. The reason we're snipers is because everyone knows Seán never misses. He never misses. Not with his catapult. Not with his cocked right arm. Not with the hurl he's cradling to his chest like a small Daniel Boone with his rifle. This is what everyone believes.

I don't believe it because it is a lie.

The real reason that me and Seán are up in this big tree is because I volunteered us for it. I do this because when Seán's playing, he's like Nicky Sullivan only worse. When one army tries to invade the other's camp, sometimes people start wrestling or stabbing with invisible bayonets. When this happens Seán sometimes loses the run of himself. He's only ten but in the middle of this do-or-die struggle, in the middle of this flail where no one shouts 'Ya missed', Seán can't hold back. It's as if the world in his head and the world where everyone else lives are all tangled up together. For Seán, it's like things leak from one to the other without anything getting in the way. So Seán stands there, with his hurl hefted like an axe and he's the centre of a slowly expanding circle of empty space.

And then Nicky Sullivan starts to cry.

This is why I take Seán up into the tree.

The tree is this huge old conker tree that grows in the corner of Stafford's field. It's easy to climb because its bark is ancient and fissured and full of handholds. It's like someone has covered the trunk in wrinkled wattles of elephant hide. If you tuck your gun into your belt you can be up it in a flash. This tree stands in Stafford's field until me and Seán are twelve years old and then a man with a chainsaw and a hi-vis jacket cuts it down.

This summer though, with our rifles, me and Seán are sitting on this massive big branch and peering out through the foliage. I'm sitting with my back to the trunk and the world around me is a sphere of green. Around me leaves overlap and spill, spreading like splayed hands. Each of these green hands hangs broken-wristed and drooping in the sunlight, swamping me, swamping Seán, swaming us, in shadow. Seán sits, straddling the branch with his bare calves and ankles twined together to steady himself. Along the back of one of his legs, briar scratches are red on white. Like raspberry ripple ice-cream. We are fifteen feet off the ground and every breath we take is vital with the cut-grass joy of summer.

I'm sitting with my back to the trunk and an ant is crawling across the back of my hand. I'm not looking at the ant though. What I am looking at is Seán. He's sitting with his back to me but there's a set to his too-square shoulders that, even at ten years old, I've learned to recognise. Beneath his T-shirt, Seán's too-big muscles are making one solid block of his torso and I just know that his broad face is horribly vacant. Looking at Seán now would be like looking into a marl hole. The hurl he's holding rocks gently in his grasp. Rhythmic as a pulse.

I'm looking at Seán's back and I'm thinking the walls have come down in his head again.

From fifteen feet up through gaps in the leaves you can see an awful lot. You can see the Blackstairs, bruise purple against the sky, the slopes of Mount Leinster diffuse in the heat haze. You can see Stafford's farmhouse with its whitewashed walls glaring from out of the browns and rust-reds of its yard. You can see mile after mile of fields and woods, all sutured and stitched together by the dark olive seaming of ditches and hedgerows. You can see all this and you can see the bumbling form of Cha Whelan making his way towards our tree.

Cha's wearing a white T-shirt with a picture of Homer Simpson on it. Homer is scratching his ass and eating a doughnut. He also looks weirdly out of proportion because Cha's cumulous puppy fat has stretched the T-shirt into widescreen format. Cha is wading through the long grass along the ditch and in his right hand he carries a Wild West Winchester. A roll of caps licks up from the Winchester's cocked hammer.

I watch Cha coming and I know that Seán is watching him too. Seán has stilled. Even the metronome of his hurl's rocking has stopped. I'm sitting there watching Seán watching Cha and I know something's going to happen. This is like all those times playing football.

The sweaty ball of lipids that is Cha Whelan is now standing in the shadow of our sniper's nest. He's fifteen feet below us and maybe ten feet to our left. Seán is still as a gravestone but I can feel the potential in him. It is static before a thunder storm. I can feel this and now I'm thinking I'd better do something. But before I can raise my plastic M16, before I can shout *bang*, before I can twitch a muscle, Seán is moving.

Seán moves calmly and quietly but with shocking speed. You know those nature programmes or documentaries you see on the BBC or Discovery? I saw this one documentary where this hippy dude from California thought he was a grizzly bear. He lived out in the Alaskan wilderness and tried to commune with these huge big monsters of animals. You're watching this documentary and you know, you just know, that the bears are going to eat him. The bears ate him. When a grizzly charges it moves like an avalanche. Soundless, inexorable and faster than it looks. Seán moves like that.

Seán's right hand lets go of the hurl and buries itself deep into the pocket of his shorts. When it comes back out it's curled around the bitter, green lump of a crab apple. The crab apple is smaller than a golf ball and its sour hardness is held cocked above Seán's right shoulder and then Seán lets loose and then Cha Whelan starts to cry.

To this day I don't know why Seán does this anymore than I know why Seán does anything. I don't know why he lets fly with all the strength in his ten-year-old's body. I don't know why he follows the crab apple's trajectory with the rapt concentration of an animal. I don't know why my shout of warning comes just late enough for Cha to look up and be caught square between the eyes. I only know that as soon as Cha's hands drop his rifle and leap to his face like horrible pale spiders, Seán starts to smile. I can see Seán in profile and I can see his liverstrip lips curl darkly at their corners. I can see him blink once, blink twice and then the smile vanishes and he turns away.

Beneath us, Cha is wailing with his hands pressed to his fore-head. His flesh is so padded that each knuckle of his fingers is a dimple rather than a bump. They look like buttons sewn into plump cushions. From under his hands, Cha's tears are rolling over the undulations of his cheeks.

Cha's wailing and he looks up at us and he goes, 'I'm telling my Mammy!'

Then he's picking up his Winchester and then he's running away.

In front of me, Seán is ignoring him. Seán is again cradling his hurl and his attention is focused God knows where. It's as if nothing's happened. It's as if someone has taken a scalpel and cleanly excised the last five minutes. It's as if nothing's happened except that all the tension, all the potential, has evaporated out of Seán. He no longer sits square-shouldered and taut. He no longer bristles.

I'm looking down to where the crab apple sits nestled in a clump of cow parsley. I'm looking at Seán and I'm saying, 'Why did you do that?'

Without turning around, Seán goes, 'I don't know.'

I can hear the confusion in him. I can hear the awareness. Again he says, 'I don't know.'

This is six years ago and this is the first time I ever see Seán hurting anyone or anything on purpose. Out of what anyone who isn't me or Seán would call *badness*. This is six years ago and this is just after his Mam walks out on him and things start to go downhill for Seán. This is six years ago and I'm sitting in a tree, watching Seán's big back and two days later Seán's trying to pretend that he doesn't have a black eye.

A couple of days after I take the O'Hara's puppy off Seán, I'm at soccer training. It is around eight o'clock and it's black dark so we've got the floodlights on. My club can only afford to have floodlights along one side of the pitch and they're mounted on these old, grey telephone poles. This means that we can only train on one half of the pitch while the other side is a swamp of black ink. The floodlights are these incredibly bright supernovas of things and they light the training area with a cold, white brilliance. They turn the world into calico and black. They turn the world into a negative.

Because the light is so harsh and uneven it's very hard to do ball work. As soon as the ball goes above the arc of the lights it simply disappears and even if you keep it on the deck it's only lit on one side, like a half moon. This means an awful lot of shuttle runs. An awful lot of sit-ups. An awful lot of laps.

I am a goalkeeper and I don't like this stuff. I don't see the point. What difference does it make whether I can do twenty laps when the longest distance I'll have to run in a game is twenty yards?

This is a source of much contention at the moment, and me and Rory, the other keeper, are almost at the point of open rebellion.

We're sitting in the moth-haunted glare of a floodlight, the soles of our boots touching and we're passing a ball to and fro, gloved hands to gloved hands. It's basically a form of sit-ups just with a ball included. In the eye of the floodlight my breath is a billowy ghost and I can hear Rory groan as he raises himself off the wet grass. I can feel the mud and the cold and the water soaking through my shorts. This is a joke altogether.

I'm thinking this and I must say something because Rory, he goes, 'I agree. We should say something.'

I'm going, 'What do you want us to say?' Every syllable is given a nebulous form by the cold and hangs in the air for a moment, suspended and ashen.

Rory's brow wrinkles and shadow masks his face and swills his right eye socket with black. Then he goes, 'We should tell him this training's fucking useless for keepers and we want to do our own stuff.'

I'm imagining Peter Cullen's reaction to two sixteen-year-olds questioning his managerial skills and I go, 'Jesus, Rory. We'll have to think of a better way of putting it than that.'

Rory says, 'You got a fucking A in English. You think of something.'

Things haven't been the same between me and Rory since last Halloween and that trip up to Dublin. The fact that I know what his brother Davey gets up to is stuck between us like a shred of beef between two molars.

I'm sitting in the wet and the cold and I'm looking at Rory and I'm trying to think of something.

Rory's just sitting there with a sour expression on his face.

We pass the ball to and fro between us. To and fro until our sixteen-year-old stomachs are aching and our breath voids into the air in a cloud of grey and a series of grunts like we're taking a dump.

Now I'm thinking, enough is enough. The ball that Rory goes to pass me misses my left shoulder and goes skittering off into the dark. Now I'm getting up and now I'm walking towards Peter Cullen and behind me I can hear Rory going, 'Thank fuck for that.'

Peter Cullen is standing in the middle of a bedlam of players. Their drills involve a lot of passing and a lot of running and each player slops and slips and is spattered with mud. Under the bright lights the spatters of mud look black like holes, like dried blood. Peter Cullen is standing there and around him the only sounds are the slap and suck of running boots and the pants and hacking curses of the boys. He's standing there watching the boys work through their drills and the scouring beam of a floodlight paints his shadow out behind him.

I'm pissed off and I walk straight up to him and I go, 'Peter, can I talk to you for a minute?'

Without turning around, without taking his eyes off the lads and their passing, he goes, 'Yeah, you can. What's up?'

Still not turning around he roars, 'Take a touch, Andy, for fuck's sake!'

Still looking at the back of his head I'm saying, 'It's about the training for the keepers.'

Peter Cullen is a big man and when he turns around the rat-grey fuzz bristling over his bullet head is halo'd by the floodlights. He's a big man and when he turns around the supernova of light behind him dresses his entire front in black. His FAI tracksuit is a featureless ebony panel and the gristly knots of his fists are pale smudges at his sides. The light coming over his shoulders lines his heavy cheekbones, the damp swelling of his double chins. Standing in front of me like this there's something primal about him. He is a golem of mud and sweat and darkness.

In the set of his shoulders, in the balling of his fists, I can see he's angry.

What I'm thinking is *ohshitohshitohshitohshitohshit* but what I'm saying is, 'Me and Rory were talking and—'

Like a brick through glass, his voice shatters my words. He's speaking low but there's an edge to what he says. It is saw-toothed and rasping and he's saying, 'Oh, talking were you? I've seen the two of you sitting on your arses all evening. Have you a problem with my training? Would you rather be running with the rest of the lads?'

I can see he's pissed off at something but I've gone too far to stop now, so I go, 'That's the point. What good is it having me and

Rory doing hours of fucking stamina work, when what we need is handling and speed drills?'

I say this a bit too loudly and a couple of the other lads stop their training and are starting to look at us. Paul notices this and his big cannonball head turns to them and he goes, 'The fucking keepers think they're too good to do the same training as the rest of us.'

I'm raising my hand up to block some of the floodlight's glare and I can't believe he's fucking said that. I'm looking from him to the boys and back again and I know how I must look, spot-lit like a fucking urchin in a play of Oliver Twist. I'm looking from him to the boys and I'm going, 'That's not what I said.'

Now all the other lads have stopped and they're standing in a line looking at me and Paul. Their breaths are coming hard and hissing through the sieves of their teeth and their heads and shoulders are wreathed in opaque, misty ribbons. I'm thinking, Paul Cullen's a bit of a bastard.

And then I'm thinking, where the fuck has Rory disappeared to?

I'm facing Paul and the rest of the lads and I can feel every single gaze fastening onto me. The lads are all gasping and blowing and under their jerseys their chests are heaving. I'm standing there, watching them watching me and I'm suddenly aware that I'm not out of breath.

I'm suddenly aware of this and then I'm going, 'Ah, for fuck's sake.'

Paul's looking at me and out of the black nothing of his face he says, 'If you don't want to train like the rest of us, you can train on your own.' Then he says, 'Ten laps and then go home. I'll talk to you on Thursday.'

Just like that he turns around to the other lads and just like that I know I'm dropped for the game on Saturday.

The way the ground is now, it's hard to run. The rain over the past few days has saturated it and here and there water lies in the pitch's gouges and troughs. In the floodlights the water looks like dribbled mercury. I'm turning away from Paul and the other boys and now I'm splashing through the metallic spills. I can feel my boots sink into the slick mud, I can feel it shifting beneath me as I start to jog. With each step there's a retching slurp and my studs carry away a cloying splat of the pitch's surface. With each step the mud mounts my boots and with each step I'm carrying a little more weight. I know that by the end of the tenth lap if I'm able to haul my feet out of the gloop at all, I'll be lucky.

On the way past Rory, he gives me this apologetic look and shrugs at me.

I'm thinking, thanks a fucking bunch you dick. I'm thinking, if you're that fucking sorry you should be doing these laps with me.

The ghost light of the floodlights runs in a salt-white band most of the way up one side of the pitch. This means that as I jog, I'll be able to see where I'm going for only about half the way round. The other side of the pitch has a black curtain drawn across it. Now, though, the floodlights are drenching me down one side and alongside me, instead of Rory, my shadow keeps pace with me. It is elongated and made spidery by the angle of the lights and it is as black as I feel. It is rank and frustrated. It is a spillage of anger.

I'm jogging up the sideline, away from Paul Cullen, away from Rory, away from the other lads and their curses and panting, away from their clutching stares. I'm jogging up the sideline and my breathing is a sea in storm and every slap and suck of my boots pulls a little more out of the muscles in my legs.

Halfway round the first lap, I look up and across the pitch at everyone else in a welter of movement under the eyes of the lights. Everyone is running and swerving and everyone is hard-edged and stark. From over here in the dark it all looks so alien. It is all dance and ritual. Primitive.

I'm on my third pass through the black when I look down to see where I'm putting my feet.

I'm on my third pass through the black when Seán grabs me by the throat.

He's looking at me and even in what little light there is I can see an awful glee in his face.

I don't know how long Seán's been waiting in the black dark beside the pitch. I don't know how long he's sat with the water dripping off the briars onto his head and neck. I don't know how long he's been watching me slop and strain in the mud with that disgusting look on his face. I don't know how long it took for his hands to get this cold and hard, how long it took for his blonde hair to get this plastered to his head, how long it took his olive green jacket to get this soaked. I don't know how long it took before the fire in his eyes exploded into life like this.

But it has and now Seán has me by the throat and before I can even yell out, he's bringing his wide, wriggling mouth close to my ear. His clammy cheek is pressed against mine and he whispers two words.

He whispers, 'Help me.'

I'm blinking in the darkness and Seán is so close to me that the smell of him fills my senses. Shampoo, Lynx deodorant and something else. Something pervasive and unpleasant. Something coming from his hands. I can feel the soft dampness of his cheek against mine. I can feel the hot surge of his breath against my ear and I can feel the way he's shaking where he stands.

I push him away from me and now I'm staring at him in the dim light from the far side of the pitch. His huge shoulders are slumped forward like his chest is caved in and his whole body is shivering in horrible little ripples. He looks shattered. In the cold wash of light from the training area he looks beaten.

He looks like this until you see his face.

His stooped shoulders have brought his head down and forwards like he's wearing an invisible yoke. He's looking at me from under his blonde eybrows and the will-o'-the-wisps that live in his eyes are frantic and bright. From between the tight curves of his lips his teeth show white and slippery. From behind this horrible smile his voice comes soft and pleading like from a different person, 'Help me.'

I'm looking at him and it's like watching someone wearing a mask.

I'm looking at him and I'm thinking, Seán's fucked. He's done something really, really bad.

I'm thinking this but what I'm saying is, 'It'll be fine. Don't be worrying. You'll be alright.'

And now Seán's expression is starting to fold into that of a sobbing child. I'm watching his smile slacken and wilt into a sagging line and I know that whatever effort he was putting into stopping himself doing bad things was way too much for him in the end. Dr Thorpe's little lipstick-red tablets didn't work and now looking at Seán I know that whatever it cost him has cost him everyting.

Standing there in the dark I'm thinking, Seán's beyond fixing.

Without really knowing what I'm doing, I put my arm around Seán's shoulders and now I'm guiding him around the black edge of the pitch. I don't how I know it but I know that I can't let any of the lads see Seán like this.

The dressing rooms are twin cubes of gulag grey. They were supposed to be hooked up to the ESB last year but that didn't happen. Now they're dark cavities of cold concrete. Useless light-bulbs dangle from the ceilings, like dead planets hanging in the void. Away from the lights, away from the slap and suck of the training, the dressing rooms are empty apart from me and Seán. Around us the coiled piles of the lads' kit-bags and clothes are little heaps of matt black in the sort of grainy charcoal that passes for light in here.

In this no-colour light I'm watching Seán as he slumps onto one of the benches lining the walls and sobs slither out of his mouth. His face is buried in his hands and now my eyes have adjusted to the gloom enough to see a hanging festoon of snot and spit arcing down from his big fingers. Under the cold wet of my jersey I can feel the cold wet of my skin, and under my skin I can feel the hot gush of my heart's every pulse.

'What happened, Seán?' I ask.

I don't like the detachment that's entered my voice. I sound like I'm trying to talk someone down from a ledge.

In the damp-concrete night of the dressing room my breath floats out from my face and away in a cloud of condensation. Seán's head is bandaged round in the moist coils of his own despair. His breath billows through the cage of his fingers like he's a trapped animal.

Now I'm moving toward him, my studs chattering on the hard cement of the floor. They sound like tapshoes, brittle and clattering and for some reason they always, always, remind me of that sound your tooth makes just as the dentist finds it with his pliers. Like something splintering.

Above the splintering of my footsteps just as I get near him, Seán goes, 'You can't tell anyone.'

His face is still in his hands so to the crown of his head I say, 'That depends, Seán. I can't promise you anything until you tell me what's wrong.'

Fighting his sobs, he lifts his head and his eyes are the first things I see. They swallow the world. It's like all the heartache, all the self-disgust that lives within Seán is now puddled in the holes of his eyes. They are bottomless shafts filled with an endless, aching dark. Looking into them it's like I'm looking into Seán and all that I see in him is a hungry universe of nothingness.

But from these blank, black sinkholes a whole world of tears is sluicing down his face. His lank hair is plastered across his forehead and his mouth is whorled about with deep lines of grief. His lips are working now but nothing's coming out except for drool and this weird gurgling sound he's making. Words want to get out of his throat but Seán's too shattered to let them.

I kneel down in front of him and I can feel the mud caking to my legs crack and chasm and tug at the hairs on my calves and thighs. I can feel the damp grit of the floor beneath my kness. The studs of my boots scrape the concrete and score lines across it.

I'm looking into the swallowing dark of Seán's eyes and I go, 'It's me, Seán. You can tell me. We always help each other. You're my best friend.'

Seán snorts a clotted ball of phlegm back up into his sinuses and he reaches his big paw out to catch the front of my jersey.

His slack mouth works without any words for a second and then he says, 'I can't tell you. You don't want me for a friend. Nobody wants me for anything. I'm a fucking freak.

And then he untangles his fist from my jersey and he hits himself in the forehead so hard I'm surprised I don't see blood.

I'm reaching for his arm and I catch it on the second attempt but at the same time I'm turning my head to look out through the gap in the metal shuttering that covers the windows. Through the slot in the sheet steel I can see the caustic light of the training area and in my head I can see the lads coming back and finding us like this. Me and Seán, me covered in mud and sweat, Seán covered in tears and snot. They'd ask a lot of questions that Seán is in no state to answer. Me neither come to think of it.

I'm thinking, if the lads come back, Seán's going to look like a weirdo. I'm thinking this and a little Judas voice in the back of my head goes *and you'll look like a fucking weirdo too with your fancy fucking words and your too-good-for-us fucking attitude. You with your psycho fucking friend.* That voice is starting to get a lot more frequent lately. That Judas screech. It terrifies me. Never before, never, have I been ashamed of Seán. I've never cared what people thought about him. He's my best friend and that means something.

Thinking this, trying to strangle the Judas screech, hanging on to Seán's hawser of an arm, I'm going, 'For fuck's sake, Seán, don't be such a handicap. Tell me what the fuck is wrong before the lads get back and kick the shit out of both of us.'

Seán stills then. He goes quiet. Not limp but motionless.

'I can't tell you,' he says. 'It's too bad.'

And then his face collapses and his whole body loosens like a landslide and his eyes start spilling tears again. And through lips that are in spasm, his voice comes clabbered and soured with self-disgust.

'I can't tell you,' he says again. 'But I can show you.'

Seán's not stupid and he's not some kind of monster. Let me get that straight. Me and him have known each other for so long now that all our memories are shared. I used to be friends with him because I didn't know how different he was. Then I was friends with him because once you're friends with someone you can't just not be friends with them. Especially when they've done nothing bad on you. Especially when they need you because they've nobody else. No Mam. A Da sliding away like grease in a fire.

There's this girl in school. Jennifer O'Riordan. *Jenny*. She is far and away the best-looking girl in school. I think so anyway. A lot of the lads think so too and they know I'm head-over-heels about her. For months I get slagged at training and once someone stuck a drawing of two stick figures having anatomically incorrect sex into my kit bag. One was labelled *Jenny* with a big clumsy arrow scrawled in the direction of the stick figure with the giant boobs and the other one was obviously supposed to be me. I know it was Brendan Currane who masterminded this because he always does his Js the wrong way round. The retard.

This is last year when we were doing our Junior Cert and I'm finding myself staring at Jenny O'Riordan during class. A lot of teachers make us sit in alphabetical order and because my second name begins with a D I'm usually stuck up in the top half of the class while she's usually behind me somewhere. Seán sits on his own because he doesn't really like anyone except me sitting beside him.

The school furniture consists of brown desks clad in a sort of slippery, fake wood veneer and brown plastic chairs that totter on the flexing tubular steel of their legs. You have to lie the chairs on their sides and straighten the legs before every class, the tubular steel is so kinked at the bends. The sixth years are too heavy for them and, if they've been in class before you, when you swivel in your seat you can feel the cheap steel start to give.

Last year I find myself doing stupid things in class so that I can catch even a glimpse of Jenny O'Riordan. I turn around in my seat for no reason. I borrow pens from people behind me even though my pencil case has a blue pen, a red pen, a HB pencil and a full mathematical set in it. It's gotten so bad at one stage that Mrs Prendergast keeps me back to talk to me about my attention span. I have never been kept back before and all the lads *oooooooohhhh* at this. My neck and face are radiating heat and for the rest of the day I can feel a red stain swimming under my skin.

Now and then Jenny will catch my eye as I'm contorting like a fucking circus act in my chair and she will smile at me. She will smile at me and there's an expression on her face when she does this that I can't quite fathom. It's like someone looking at a baby or something. But as far as I'm concerned a smile is a smile and on each occasion I'm gurning back at her like a simpleton.

This all comes to a head one day in Maths.

I'm shit at sums and I start thinking about how Jenny looks with her head bent over her copy, the blonde curtain of her hair tucked behind her ear and the white nubs of her teeth nipping at the end of her pencil. Mr Fogarty isn't paying much attention to the class. He's doing something with the roll, his face wrinkled beneath his dome of slick, hairless, pale skin. It's like his entire head is a ball of scar tissue. His control over his classes is absolute. His discipline is a beartrap thing of sudden cruelty. The only noises in his room are the scratching of pencils and the chitinous clicking of calculators.

Like something out of a pantomime, I'm flicking little stilletto glances around me under my brows before I elbow my red pen off the desk with all the finesse of a fat man falling off a high stool. Mr Fogarty looks up at me. Only his eyes move. His head stays bowed but his eyes move and his gaze travels from me to the fallen red pen and back to me again. His upper lip wrinkles in silent contempt and he goes back to his work.

Smiling inanely I lean out of my chair and smiling inanely I turn my head to catch Jenny's eye.

She lifts her face and for a long moment we are locked together, she staring at me, me suspended awkwardly over the edge of the chair, my body torqued out into space.

The chair creaks once before the legs give way and the class explodes into laughter. One creak. Like it was jeering me.

At big break Seán says, 'You have to say something to her.'

We're in the gym and the place is an echoing church of laughter and conversation. I'm looking at him over the rumpled, golden hump of a chicken goujon roll. Around a mouthful of dough, ketchup and reconstituted chicken gloop, I go, 'What are you talking about?'

I'm still embarrassed about what happened in Maths this morning and the last thing I want to do is go anywhere near Jenny O'Riordan for the rest of the day. I can picture her hand coming up to hide the laughter that sings in her eyes and shakes her shoulders. I can picture the hilarity on her face as Mr Fogarty hauls me off the floor by the collar.

I lost my fucking pen as well.

Seán looks at me with his big, blank eyes and he says slowly, like he's thinking hard about every syllable, 'You have to say something to her. Everyone saw that you were staring at her when you fell. Everyone sees you every day staring at her. I can hear everyone saying that you're dying about her.'

I'm swallowing my mouthful of carbohydrates and pretend chicken and I'm going, 'Ah, for fuck's sake. Is everyone talking about us?'

Seán looks at me and his lips squirm in a weird smile and he says, 'Why do you say "us"?'

He says, 'They are talking about you. Not Jenny. You don't have an "us".'

I look at him for a moment that stretches into a long expanse of silence. Everyone else is having their lunch too and the silence between us is filled with other people's laughter and monkey-house chatter. He's right of course. There is no 'us' when it comes to me and Jenny. The admission of this is hooked into my bowels.

I'm shaking my head because I'm an idiot. I'm shaking my head and then I'm saying, 'Yeah.'

And then I go, 'Just don't you start taking the piss as well.'

Seán looks at me then with his great heavy face and he says, 'I won't take the piss. I don't ever take the piss. Even when all the others were laughing at you, I wasn't.'

I look back at him and I'm thinking *all the others?* but what I'm saying is, 'Thanks, man.'

Seán beams like I've just given him the greatest compliment he's ever gotten.

We spot Jenny sitting with two friends on one of the low windowsills lining the corridor that links the old and new parts of the school. She is wrapped all about by the fall of sun through the glass and her hair has ignited into gold filigree. Herself and her friends don't even look up as we stop in front of them. They are looking at Jenny's iPhone and the scratchy, parched audio from the video they're watching skitters all along the corridor.

I don't know what to do and I'm looking at Seán. Seán shrugs and nods dumbly toward Jenny like he's fucking Lassie or something.

Not knowing what to do I clench and unclench my fists and not knowing what to do I make this stupid polite cough.

One of Jenny's friends, a fat girl with hair like unravelled Brillo Pads, lifts her big head and looks at me like I'm something she's scraped off her shoe. She sneers at us and goes, 'What do you two losers want?'

I blink at this and I say, 'Can I have a word with Jenny please?'

I'm saying this and at the same time I'm thinking, why the fuck am I asking permission?

Jenny's not looking at me. And Jenny not looking at me goes, 'Tell him I don't want to talk to him.'

The fat girl says, 'She doesn't want to talk to you.'

Again I look at Seán. He's grinning encouragingly and he's nodding eagerly at me. Now I'm looking from Jenny to her slab-of-lard friend and now I'm going, 'Look, I don't need an interpreter. Jenny, do you have a minute?'

Jenny looks up at me and she smiles and she goes, 'Why? Do you want to show me how you can fall on your arse again?'

That thing that was hooked in my guts, the one that snagged there when I admitted that Jenny and I weren't an 'us', that thing now rips free and unspools my innards. Jenny is smiling so sweetly that she's threatening to give the entire school diabetes and my whole belly is opening up with a long agonising yawn. Both of Jenny's friends are laughing at me and I'm thinking that this is what Daniel O'Hara must have felt like with his Mam boxing the back off him and the whole school sniggering at him.

I'm standing there like something built out of wet clay and I don't know what to do. The expressions scuttling across the girls' faces are awful things, cruel and in flux and all of a sudden every

44

atom of me feels like it's being dissolved by their scorn. In the middle of the corridor I'm standing there and I feel like my entire being has become a big blank naught.

And then Seán says something.

He stands beside me and he goes, 'You're not very nice people.'

Jenny bridles and her chin tucks into her neck. Her fat friend lifts her hand, index finger quivering upright in a daytime TV *oh no you di'ant* gesture of indignation, and she says, 'What business is it of yours, you fucking ape?'

But Seán is on a roll now and his voice just rumbles straight over fatso's talk-show performance. He's going, 'You're not very nice people. My friend is the nicest person in this school and you people are horrible. I don't like you. You just talk about people all the time. You're always mean. All the time you're mean. You make all the other girls cry.'

Then he lifts his big hand and he points at Jenny. His voice just keeps coming out of his mouth gathering momentum and speed like a tsunami.

Now, still pointing at Jenny, he's saying, 'You like to keep these two around you because they're not as good-looking as you. You always want everyone to look just at you. If people aren't looking at you, you disappear. I see the way you keep looking at your own self in the windows. You have a mirror in the lid of your maths set too. You're friends with ugly people because you want to stand out. You don't even like them. You talk about them behind their backs.'

Jenny looks appalled but Seán just keeps going. Now his spar of an arm has swung to point at Jenny's friends and he's saying, 'And you two only hang around with her because you think that people will look at her and see you. But they don't. They see Jenny and her ugly friends. And you know it and you cry yourself to sleep knowing it.'

His arm finally lowers and his voice slows and he says, 'You're all horrible people. You're not really friends so you try to make everyone else feel as horrible as you do.'

He stops then and he mumbles, 'Friends don't do things like that. Friends are nice.'

The three girls all sit with their mouths open and you can actually feel the tension between them. The slimmer of Jenny's friends, her nose a fleshy hook overhanging her mouth, is going bright bright red. The truth in Seán's words has tugged at something raw between them and over the next few weeks everyone notices that Jennifer O'Riordan finds herself more and more on her own.

That's my friend Seán. Like I said, he's not stupid and he's not some kind of a monster.

In the dark it's hard to peel myself out of my football gear and tog back into my clothes. My skin is slick and clammy and every fibre of my football gear clings to me like it's feeding off me. I'm sitting on a wooden bench and I'm trying to yank my socks on over the cold blocks of my feet. Seán is standing in the dark sniffing and dragging his sleeve across his face.

I look at him and then I'm going, 'Any chance of a bit of light? Use your phone or something.'

Seán blinks at me. Even in the dark I can see his white lids flicker down over the inky pools of his eyes, blotting them out like petals on black water. Now he's shrugging and now he's saying, 'I don't have it. Da took it on me.'

I stop with my sock half on and my shoulders slumping forward and I go, 'Why did he do that?'

Seán shrugs again and he says, 'He says I'm not getting it back until I cop on. It's quare annoying.'

He says this last in a flat voice of dead lead. He couldn't sound less annoyed if he tried. I'm thinking, that's what Seán knows you should say when your Da takes your phone on you. *Annoyed* is how you should feel.

Then he goes, 'Where's yours? I'll hold it for you.'

I'm struggling with my jeans now and I say to him, 'Why would I bring my phone to training? I don't even have any money on me. They don't lock these dressing rooms.'

Seán nods, slowly and deliberately and says, 'So we're in the dark?'

I smile up at him and I go, 'We're used to it.'

We sneak out of the dressing rooms. Off to our left the lads are all still slogging their slog on a patch of grass that they've churned to quag. The floodlights are dousing the scene with a bitter light and the cold smoke of their body heat haunts their every move and footstep. Paul Cullen is a black crepe cut-out against the light. His voice bells out and drowns out all the slopping, all the squelching, all the panting, all the parched whooping for breath.

The driveway leading from the pitch is covered in loose chippings of this hard grey stone that's flecked with little winking dots of quartzite. This means that as we walk away from the pitch and Paul Cullen's training session we kick sprays of gravel out in a fan and we leave shallow gouges in the carpet of stones behind us. The only noises are our breathing, the rattle of my gear bag and the steady hiss and crunch of our footsteps. As you get to the bottom of the driveway you start to hear the sounds of traffic and a haze of orange light starts to filter across the stones from the sodium arcs angling over the road. The lights are at the end of these long arms that jut out perpendicular to the lampposts just like the gallows you draw when you play hangman. In their Halloween-orange light Seán is the biggest and saddest munchkin in the whole chocolate factory.

I look hard at his profile and I say, 'Seán, you have to tell me what's wrong.'

He's ignoring me and his great liquid eyes are studiously avoiding mine. He wags his head like a cart horse yoked under a huge weight and says, 'I can't tell you. It's too hard. I'll show you the camp. Then you'll see.'

I can feel the unease creep back into me. It's sliding under my skin until my skin feels taut and gelid. I'm frowning now and I'm going, 'What camp?'

Seán doesn't say anything. He just keeps plodding onward, his head rocking on its thick neck.

When we get to the road Seán turns right. This takes us away from town and out toward the Milehouse. I stop just as Seán starts to walk out along this road. He's about two yards in front of me and his back is a broad orange and black wall under the road lighting. I can see the still-wet fabric of his army surplus jacket stretch across the drumlin mounds of his deltoid muscles. I don't know why Seán wants to walk out the Milehouse Road at quarter-to-nine at night. I don't know what he's done to scare and disgust him so much that his throat closes and he nearly gags when he tries to tell me. I don't know what this camp of his is. All I know is that I'm suddenly a bit scared.

And in the back of my head Judas gibbers, *Another fucking first.*

Without looking at me he's saying, 'It's not far. It's not even as far as the school.'

I stare at his back for longer than I probably mean to and then I'm saying words and I'm hating the whine that they come out in. I'm saying, 'If I'm too late, Da's going to fucking murder me. I don't even have my phone.'

Seán turns around then and in his face I see an enormous sadness. It's like his whole big frame is one giant cistern of tears. Picture how you'd feel if every bad thing you thought about yourself was suddenly proved to be true. Every failing, every flaw was there in front of you clear as day. Everything unvarnished and burred with ragged edges and all slimed over with failure. Can you picture how you'd look? Well, this is how Seán looks. I see all this in Seán.

He says, 'Please.'

Looking at him I heft my gear bag, and looking at him I'm going, 'Ah, fuck it. Go on. Da won't mind that much.'

For a moment it's like Seán is going to smile but he doesn't. Instead he just turns around and starts heading on up the road to where the lights run out and the dark chokes the road between ditches the same colour as Seán's jacket.

With every step away from town it's like he's drawing further and further into himself like a neutron star slowly caving in. With every step Seán is becoming a black hole. He's not saying anything and he's not looking at anything and he's sucking all the light and life from around us. The whole world is background to Seán's misery.

I don't say anything. I have nothing to say. Whatever Seán wants to show me he'll show me and then we can decide what to do about it. I hope, I really hope, that the guards can be kept the fuck out of it. I also hope that there's some other brand of tablets that Dr Thorpe can put Seán on. The little red ones, they aren't worth a curse.

About a hundred yards after the lights die out there's this big ragged tear in the footpath and this big ragged tear in the ditch. The tears are the works entrance to one of those half-finished estates that stagger up out of muddy fields and dirty lakes of rainwater all over the country. All over the place there's ragged concrete boxes, empty as rotten teeth and they chew the sky and collect rain and empty cans and their rebar rusts and colours the puddles like blood.

The gap in the ditch leading to this particular jumble of abandoned concrete is sealed off through the foolproof expedient of throwing two steel mesh barriers across it. No locks. No chains. Just two galvanised lattices of mesh propped up against the briar-scrawled banks on the left and right and sagging in a pathetic V where they meet in the middle. If you look up and to one side, in the ditch above this impenetrable barrier you can see a broken advertising hoarding with a computer-generated image of three-bedroom-semis and lime-green-grass and smiling computer-generated-familes and everything's hyphenated with all the joined-up-thinking. Where the name of the estate should be someone's taken a spray can and graffiti'd the word COCK in four-foot-high letters.

Seán stops at the gap in the ditch and still not saying anything he pushes his way through the hole between the wire mesh and the snarl of briars that covers it. I follow him and I can feel my runners sink into the morrass of Caterpillar-chewed mud that is the ground beyond. There's not much of a moon and I can't see a thing and I'm floundering around before Seán grabs my arm and steadies me.

I go, 'What are we doing here, Seán? This is fucking insane.'

Seán, in the dark, goes, 'We're nearly there. It's the second one on the right.'

In front of us there's a row of half-finished houses. Even in the dim illumination of moon-rind and light pollution from the town I can see that they look like something you see on the news. They look like a street scene from Iraq or Afghanistan, windowless and austere. They look bombed out.

Me and Seán, we slew and slip across the wet yards of mud until we stand in front of one particular shell of a house. There's nothing that sets it apart from the others. The window frames are just as empty and the door is an open yawn of midnight just like all the rest.

I'm thinking all this but then something catches in my throat. Right on the edge of certainty, right so's I'm not sure whether I actually smell something or not, I think I get a reek of something. And just like that I'm back beside the pitch and Seán's big paws have me by the throat. And just like that I can smell the something else that's coming from his hands. Something pervasive and unpleasant.

Seán's looking at me and he's going, 'It's in here.'

And just like that I'm afraid. Actually really afraid.

My Mam died when I was six. I'm not saying this out of a desire for sympathy or understanding or anything like that. The fact that me and Seán haven't had a Mam for years has fuck all to do with how we turned out. I'm grand, Seán's internal wiring is badly fused. We are both ourselves. It's not anything else's fault.

My Mam died when I was six. I don't remember that much about her. The only real concrete image I have of her comes from the photos that Da looks at every so often. He takes them out of this small cardboard box and sits, not watching the TV, shuffling through snapping drifts of polaroids and landscapes, black-and-whites and old sepias. They slither in his grip like a pack of playing cards.

In all these pictures my Mam is grinning and I'm in some of them, all crumpled and grumpy. In all these pictures my Mam with her big hair and her '90s fashions looks like something out of *Reeling in the Years*. She looks like what she is. Something gone and in the past. Something from another time.

But these photos don't get across the emotion I still get when I think about her. I can't see her unless I look at the photos but I can feel her all the time.

The last proper memory I have of her is from the Strawberry Fair maybe nine or ten years ago. The Strawberry Fair is this festival that the town puts on to celebrate the joy of summer and the lovely, fat tumour of sun-blooded sweetness that is the Wexford Strawberry. Everyone always says it hasn't been the same since it left the Prom but me and the lads are too young to remember when it was anything other than shit.

I love strawberries. And I love the summer. The Strawberry Fair, however, really is terrible.

Picture the market square of any fairly big town. Now put a stage at one end and white plastic lawn furniture all around so that pensioners can sit down and eat their ice creams and kids can slalom between and drunks can stumble over. Now on this stage put either a crap DJ or some band that was big when the festival organisers were young. Overhead you dissect the sky with taut lines of purple and gold bunting. The festival organisers are baffled that people just stay in the pubs so they don't have to listen to the bad music and don't have to avoid the puddles of puke. The local scumbags deal drugs and fight and drink cans in the side streets and you always get women in old Wexford GAA jerseys strolling around. The words *Wexford Creamery* are stretched across their tits. This always cracks me up. Like everyone else, the organisers of all this are stuck twenty years behind the times. Everyone gets stuck at a certain point and then gets pissed off because the world leaves them behind. It's like every grown-up is a version of my Da. Always going through photos of stuff that doesn't exist anymore.

The last proper memory I have of my Mam is from the car park of the L&N supermarket. The festival organisers set up this huge big haunted mansion that you pay into to get the shite frightened out you by plastic skeletons and actors hamming it up in twine wigs and white face paint. The haunted mansion is actually a series of bulk cargo containers all bolted together with their insides turned into a papier-mâché tunnel with mirrors and lights and sound effects. Walking through it is like walking through the bowels of a giant worm that's swallowed the contents of a fancy dress shop and a company of terrible amateur dramatists. The outside of this block of containers is clad in plywood hoarding that's been painted in swirling purples with ghosts and goblins leering across the car park.

Even at six years old I'm wondering, what have ghosts got to do with strawberries?

My mam has me by the hand and I remember the taste of candyfloss around my mouth and the smell of melted sugar that seems to be what years-ago summers smell like. Mam is smiling down at me but the sun is behind her head and I can't see her face. She had red frizzy hair and I remember it balled around her head like a nest round an egg. All about her there's the corona of a nuclear explosion millions of miles away but right in front of me her face is a mask of black. She pays the man at the ticket counter and we go into the haunted mansion.

When we go in I remember she goes in first and a black curtain falls down behind us and everything goes pitch-black. I'm only six and I don't like this and my little hand tries to tighten on my mother's but my fingers don't go all the way around and I know that I won't be able to hold on if something bad happens.

Then something bad happens.

A strobe light explodes. It batters my eyes with whumping pulses of light and a scream like something dying comes out of a speaker right beside my head. A rubber skeleton with an unhinged jaw gets shunted toward us by a mechanical arm. You know when a rasher isn't crispy? You know when you cut into it and lift it on the oily tines of your fork? You know that bit of fat that waggles disgustingly and drips stuff onto your plate? That's how the skeleton's jaw moves. Elastic and nauseating.

And in the machine-gun brilliance of the strobe light and in the ball of feedback distortion from the fake scream my Mam lets go of me.

I remember this. Cold and hard as the flash from a strobe light, I remember this.

Her fingers loose and she steps away from me and I'm left standing there, terrified.

I'm sixteen now and I know that what happens is she gets a fright and she jumps and she lets go of my hand. I know that I'm standing there for about two seconds before she grabs me again and lifts me up into her arms. But at six years old this all pretty hard to take.

In the hammering light of the strobe it's like she's receding into the distance and all her movements are jerky and spastic. The terror that I feel isn't an emotional thing. It is in my muscles and bones. It is something physical that crushes me and buries me and scalds my throat.

This is the last proper memory that I have of my mother. Being terrified as she seems to vanish into the dark. Dread on dread.

This is the last time I'm really afraid. Actually really afraid.

Now I'm standing looking into this open sore of a half-finished house and I can feel that same fear bucking in my chest. I can feel the vomit churn in my gut. I'm looking from the empty door-frame to Seán and then back again. I can still get that weird smell. Something organic and rotten. Something that wants to sour the mucus in your throat and seed infection in your sinuses.

My tongue comes out and rasps along lips that feel like strips of leather stitched onto my face. I'm licking my lips and I'm going, 'What's in there, Seán?'

Seán shakes his big head and he goes, 'I don't want anyone else to see this. I don't know what to do.'

I look at him for a minute and he looks at me and then the two of us are walking through the empty doorframe.

Inside, the house is a cold empty cube made up of smaller cold empty cubes. None of the walls are plastered and there's ragged holes in them for wiring and fittings that will never be wired or fitted. The place is haunted by the ghost of what might have been. It is a non-existent home for a computer-generated family. The cold is so sharp in here that it straightaway sinks into your skin and penetrates your muscles. I'm still cold and still wet from training and this place is acting like a fridge so that I'm shivering only a few steps into the hallway. My breathing is coming harder and with every breath I pull more of the damp and more of the cold and more of that awful smell into my lungs.

Seán leads the way down the hall and his footsteps grind on the clammy concrete dust that powders the place. It's like wet talcum to the touch. I'm following him and I'm getting more and more uneasy with every step. The smell is getting stronger and in front of us there's the rectangular hole of what should have been a kitchen door. Seán's frame is a moving wedge of darkness and with his shoulders stooped and his head hanging he looks like something out of a horror story.

Seán stops at the threshold between the hall and the kitchen and he goes, 'It's in here. I'm really sorry. Really, really sorry.'

The kitchen at least has windows and a sliding patio door in one wall that looks out over a three-foot drop into a ditch of filthy water. Pipes prod up out of the concrete floor, prongs of plastic tubing onto which washing machines and dishwashers, sinks and tumble dryers should be slotted. Not now though. Now the fuzzy light from the town and the road filters in through the windows and makes it look like my club's dressing rooms. Migraine-grey and swamped in shadow.

Only the smell is vibrant.

A good few times, when I'm off over at my uncle's, himself and my Da are skinning rabbits. What you do is you slit the skin of the belly and kind of fold it over the knee joints of the back legs. The skin separates from the muscle underneath a lot easier than you'd think. It makes a sound like peeling velcro. Then you make a nick in the back legs. Then you break them and cut off the lucky rabbit's feet. You do this with pheasants too and you can grab the little white slippery tab of the severed tendon and pull on it. This makes the claws curl in on themselves like the dead pheasant is shaking its fist at you. When you have the skin pulled off the stubs of the back legs you can then tug it up along the back until you get to the head. All the time you're doing this you're hearing the same tearing noise of peeling velcro. Once you get the skin up to the head you can let it dangle all limp and pathetic over the rabbit's face. This always reminds me of the snotty asthmatic kid in school who gets his jumper pulled over his head. Then you cut its head off. After this you empty out its belly and the cavity under its ribs and then you wash off all the blood and all the slime and all the fluids.

The trouble is sometimes when you're doing this you catch the sac of the intestines with the point of your skinning knife. The trouble is your knife is really fucking sharp so when it snags this brown-purple sausage of gut it punches straight through it like a surgeon's scalpel. This is pretty easy to do, especially the first few times you do it. It's the smell that gets you.

The smell of punctured viscera. The smell of half-formed shit and half-digested food. The smell of violation and death and indignity.

This is the smell that fills the kitchen.

And suddenly I'm thinking, please don't let it be a person. Please don't let it be a person.

And from beside me Seán goes, 'I'm really sorry. Really really sorry.'

I'm nearly puking now but I'm saying, 'What the fuck have you done, Seán?'

Seán slides past me and into the kitchen the way on telly a big ship will slide through an oil spill. He is all weight and silence and he points into the far corner of the kitchen. He points into the far corner of the kitchen but his eyes stay fixed on the concrete floor.

Not wanting to, I follow him and stare at where he's pointing.

In the far corner of the concrete box there's what looks like a rug, all bundled up and lying in a puddle of shadow. Around this lump there are five or six other small lumps. All are lying in darkness and all are unmoving.

With my hand to my mouth I'm taking a step towards the lumps. I can't make them out in the gloom and so I'm taking another step and then another.

And then I see what they are.

There's a dead dog lying in the corner of the kitchen, lying in a slick of her own blood, lying with her dead puppies all around her. Her stomach is slit all the way open. Dead dogs litter the cold concrete floor.

When I get sick it rushes out of my mouth and just keeps on coming.

I don't know how I get outside. I don't how I turn on my heel with vomit on my chin, vomit on my lips, vomit in my throat. I don't know how I stumble along the hallway. I don't know how quickly I manage to get away from that room with its stench and its horror. All I know is that now I'm standing in the half-finished porch sucking great gulps of air through my nose and mouth and I don't know how I got here. I can smell the mud and the rain and the wet concrete. I can smell the smells of decay and abandonment. I can smell the acid stink of my own puke.

Then Seán's beside me and out of fear and anger and disgust I go, 'Don't fucking touch me! Jesus Christ what the fuck is wrong with you?'

Seán just stares at me, sadly. He knows that this is coming. He knows what people are going to say if this gets out. He knows he has done a really bad thing.

I know that he knows this and he just stares vacantly at me. The stones of his eyes are wide and round and wet in the dark.

I'm looking at him and now I'm scrubbing at my mouth with the sleeve of my jacket. I should have a bottle of water in my gear bag and I start to root around to try and find it. I have to get the smell out of my throat. I have to wash the vomit off my face. I find the bottle and the water is cold and it ripples shivers all over my body but the goosebumps aren't there from the water.

Seán watches me in silence and I stare back at him and go,

'What the fuck are we supposed to do now? Why would you do something like that?

Seán's sighing and he brings both of his big hands up to his face and then he drags them down along his cheeks. They pull his face out of shape for a moment like he's about to pull off a latex mask and not be Seán anymore.

He's sighing and he goes, 'I didn't kill her. I saw her being hit by a car. The driver didn't stop. I went over and I saw her big belly and I could feel how warm she was. I cut her open and tried to play with her pups but they wouldn't do anything. Some of them moved around for a while but then they died. I tried to put them back in—'

I'm going, 'Stop it right fucking there. You cut open a dead dog to play with the puppies? Jesus Christ. Why didn't you get a vet?'

Seán's shrugging and I know what he's going to say before he's even saying it. He says, 'They'd take the pups.'

I'm staring at him like I've lost the ability to think. I have lost the ability to think. The patchwork housing estate, the sobbing dark of the sky, everything is a confusing meaningless mess.

I'm trying to speak but words aren't coming out. I can feel my head shaking from side to side but I'm not the one doing it. It's like someone has a hold of my skull and they're twisting it this way and that, the way you hold somebody's arm and start going *stop hitting yourself stop hitting yourself*. Right now someone's doing that to my entire body.

Seán goes, 'We can't tell my Da. He'd kill us.'

And I go, 'What the fuck is this "us" shite?'

Seán is staring at me and in the dark he looks like something placid and bovine on its way to a slaughterhouse.

Still tasting my own sick in the back of my throat I'm going, 'Alright. We can't tell your Da. We can't tell mine either.'

Seán with his face sad, his hands flat against his thighs, Seán with his head down, goes, 'I don't want to do this again. I don't want to do anything like this again.'

And then, just like that, I'm going, 'Dr Thorpe.'

And then, just like that, I'm saying, 'We can tell Dr Thorpe and because he's your doctor he can't tell anyone else. We need to tell him you need new tablets. We need to tell him that the ones you're on aren't fucking working.'

I take a look back into the house and I go, 'They're really not fucking working.'

I'm not sure if I really like Dr Thorpe. I was scared of him when I was little. When Mam was dying but I was too young to realise she was dying, me and Da go down to see her in hospital. She's lying in bed not moving at all. She's lying there all snaked around in plastic tubing and a bag of clear liquid drip-drip-drips into her through an IV. With all the white and all the equipment she looks like an astronaut who's gotten all snarled up in her own gear. She's like someone drowning in the vacuum of outer space. Except she's lying on a bed drowning in the antiseptic smell of a hospital.

Driving home and I'm asking Da about whether Mam will be better soon. The rain is coming down and the world outside the car windows is one solid slab of falling grey. Da says how Mam is doing fine and that she'll be back to herself before we know it. As small as I am, I know he's lying. But I don't say anything about it and he doesn't say anything else and on the radio Liam Spratt is asking his co-commentator, Georgie

O'Connor, how he found the traffic on the way up to Croke Park.

'About the same, Liam,' says Georgie. 'I was in your car.'

Dr Thorpe used to live just before you turned off the Milehouse Road for our old house. Me and Da are walking up his drive and there's something in the way that Da's face looks that I really don't like. Then we're standing in Dr Thorpe's porch and the rain is bouncing cold spray to hit me in the shins. Shorts. I'm wearing shorts.

Dr Thorpe's doorbell goes ding-dong-ding-dong-ding-dong. Real soft. The sound is sort of woolly-edged like the sound of something whispering. Da keeps pressing the bell and he shifts from foot to foot like he really needs to pee.

Dr Thorpe's door swishes open and he stands there looking at us with his hair a solid crest above his shining face. With the door opening comes the smell of fake pine air freshener. I remember that.

Da goes, 'I'm sorry, Doctor. I'm sorry but I don't know what to do. She's in so much pain.'

He stops then and I can hear the heartbreak lodge in his throat. He is choked by sadness.

Dr Thorpe's hand is about level with my fat face and across the back of it I can see a lot of little cuts. They're all thread-thin and beaded with blood. As I'm looking he lifts his hand and sucks the cuts. For an instant when he talks there's blood all feathered across his teeth.

'We'll think of something,' he says. 'Come on in.'

Dr Thorpe's kitchen is one big cavern of amber light and

ash-blonde furniture. I swear to God it smells of cinnamon. On the kitchen table there's about a dozen pots of sapling roses. Dr Thorpe goes over to the counter beside the sink and lifts the kettle and shakes it at Da and me.

He goes, 'Tea? No?'

Da says back to him, 'Jesus, Syl, my stomach's in fucking knots.'

Neither of them look at me. It's like I don't exist anymore.

Dr Thorpe's talk-show face splits open like an over-ripe fruit dropped from a height and from his smile his voice goes, 'Okey-dokey. We'll chat about this in the other room.'

Then he turns to me and still smiling he goes, 'Can you wait here, little man?'

Even at six years of age I know this is a fucking stupid question.

Without waiting for my answer Dr Thorpe and my Da go into the sitting room. I can hear their voices all diffuse and burbling through the walls. They sound like indigestion. They sound like the workings of my guts.

I'm left standing in the kitchen and I stare and stare at the potted roses. On the one nearest the table's edge I can see little white shreds of Dr Thorpe's skin snagged on the black commas of the thorns. I remember that. I remember reaching to pluck them off. The rubbery scraps of the back of his hand.

My sinuses are clogged with the pulpy sweetness of rose petals.

Everything in the other room goes all quiet and when Dr

Thorpe and my Da come back into the kitchen I jump. Dr Thorpe is going, 'If she's let home on Saturday, I'll call round Saturday night.'

And Da's going, 'Thankyouthankyouthankyouthankyou.' He's nearly crying and snot is emptying out of his nose.

I'm watching the two of them and when Dr Thorpe says, 'This is between us and nobody else. We're all in this. Understand?' even my six-year-old ears hear that there's something not right about this.

And Da's going, 'Thankyouthankyouthankyouthankyou.'

Dr Thorpe plugs in the kettle and goes, 'Just remember. You owe me one.'

I don't know what's happening, I don't know why the adults are ignoring me and talking in code. At six-years-old I don't know all that much but I do know that Mam comes home on Saturday morning and Dr Thorpe pronounces her dead at eleven fifteen that night.

Like I said, I'm not sure if I like Dr Thorpe.

Dr Thorpe lives just down from the grotto on the Nunnery Road. There was this derelict site there for years until he bought it and built this massive big detached mansion on it. We used to play there with the lads from the council estate when we were younger but then Jarlath Gildea got in a fight with one of the older lads from the estate and we weren't allowed to play there anymore. Now there's an eight-foot wall most of the way around except where a set of big double gates opens out onto the road. There's a sign on the gates that says *Beware of the Dog*. Dr Thorpe's dog is a German Pointer like my uncle's and she's the nicest dog you'd ever meet. I don't know why he puts the sign up. Everyone knows it's a load of crap.

To get to Dr Thorpe's we, me and Seán, have to head back down the Milehouse Road and swing left and go through the estate. The estate used to be rough enough a few years back but it's mellowed these days. Everyone's gotten on a bit and lots of the older lads have moved away. There's a lot of pensioners in the estate now and a lot of the houses are actually owned and they're not the Council's anymore. It's like it's respectable all of a sudden.

We half-jog down through the estate and now we're on the Nunnery Road.

We stop to catch our breath and Seán goes, 'I'm really sorry. I'm really really sorry.'

I'm smiling at him but I know it looks watery and that I don't mean it but I'm saying, 'It's not you. I know you're sorry. We'll get you to the doctor and then it'll all be okay.'

Seán nods and smiles and he doesn't catch the desperation in my voice.

Dr Thorpe's gates have a little buzzer set into the concrete of one of the pillars. There's a little plastic panel with a light behind it that shines like sun through fog and there's this kind of speaker thing that's making this constant sort of crackling noise. Beyond the gates Dr Thorpe's big house has a light on in every window. It looks like Eldorado in the dark. Seán's standing beside me and he's shifting his weight from foot to foot and his fists are clenching and unclenching. He's nervous and angry with himself, and shame and embarrassment are reddening his face even as he's standing there.

I say, 'It's alright, Seán. He deals with people who like to stick their dicks in industrial machinery. If he can treat knob burns without passing judgement, you'll be a doddle.'

I'm grinning then because I'm trying to reassure him and then I'm punching him in the shoulder. I'm punching him in the shoulder and then I'm pressing the buzzer.

Nothing happens.

No chime. No voice. Nothing. The incessant crackling noise just keeps on crackling, not changing tone or breaking up in any way. A soft exhalation of white noise is hitting me in the face and I'm staring at the buzzer and I'm pressing it again. To anyone watching me I must look like one of those lab monkeys that have to try and solve a puzzle to get a banana.

Nothing happens. No banana for me.

Seán is frowning at me and a car rumbles past on the road, its headlights dipping so that it doesn't blind us. Nevertheless Seán turns away quickly when the car first rounds the corner and lights us up. He spins his back to the road in an awkward, drunken lurch. With the two of us standing outside Dr Thorpe's gates, me with my face shoved up close to the buzzer and Seán hiding his, we must look like the two most inept burglars on the planet. To the driver of the passing car we must look like complete scumbags.

Seán is groaning again and he's pressing his hands to his eyes. His breath is whuffling in the cupped palms of his hands and now I'm thinking, the smell from his hands. Dog's blood. Dog's blood must have gotten all over me. The stink of it. My football jersey is stained with the clotted blood and amniotic fluids of that dead dog.

I'm almost retching again and Seán's groaning words. He goes, 'I want to go home. I don't want people to see me. Everyone thinks we're freaks as it is. Don't make me.'

And I say, 'You're not going home until we get you sorted out. You need a doctor, Seán.'

Seán groans and groans and now he's rocking on his heels.

I'm thinking, for fuck's sake. I push at the gates to see if they'll slide open like on the Enterprise. They don't. They just rear in front of me solid and slippery and obsidian. The *Beware of the Dog* sign flaps on its little wire fixings and the Alsation etched into the yellow plastic looks like it's laughing at me.

And now I'm going, 'Open sesame or something you fucking piece of junk.'

I'm rattling the gates now and they're still not opening and Seán's groans are getting louder. Pretty soon someone's going to come walking along or they'll stop their car and ask us what we're doing standing here moaning and rattling the doctor's gate. Pretty soon someone's going to ask us this and then they're going to see that the dark stuff on Seán's jacket sleeves is too dark to be just rainwater and then they'll get the smell and then we're pretty much fucked.

Seán goes, 'I want to go home. Let me go home.'

I can feel every spark and flare of every synapse. I can feel the hot workings of my bowels and stomach. I'm suddenly aware of every inch of my frogbelly skin. I can feel my eyes in their sockets. They are coated with grit. I am beginning to panic and the fact that I'm pretty calmly reflecting on the fact that I'm beginning to panic doesn't help matters in the slightest.

I'm looking at Seán and then I'm looking at the gates and then I'm going, 'We could climb the wall or something.'

And Seán goes, 'I don't want to climb the wall.'

I'm pissed off now and I go, 'For fuck's sake, Seán. You're worse than a child. Do you want to go home the way you are? Do you want to explain to your Da why you're so worked up?'

I'm snarling at him and I hate the rasp that's in my voice. I hate that the years of being Seán's only friend have bred in me this amount of venom. Every time I've had to make an excuse. Every time I've had to cover for him. It all bubbles through my words.

I'm saying, 'I'm not leaving you on your own, Seán. Not until I can get you sorted. I don't trust you.'

Seán looks like I've kicked him in the stomach.

I'm looking at him looking at me with his big soft head and I'm thinking, we haven't got time for this crap. I'm thinking this and then I'm going, 'We're climbing the fucking wall and that's it.'

And, just like that, Seán goes, 'Okay.'

The wall around Dr Thorpe's house is eight feet high and built out of concrete blocks. Dr Thorpe hasn't gotten round to painting it yet and so the blocks make one big expanse of abrasive grey.

Here and there moss and tiny little plants with loveheart leaves make green smears on the dead stone and cement. I'm looking at the wall and then I'm looking up and down the road and then I'm going, 'You go up first. I'll give you a boost and then you can pull me up after.'

Seán looking hurt shakes his head and Seán still looking hurt goes, 'I'll drop you.'

Now I'm sighing and I'm going, 'You won't drop me. I didn't mean to say I didn't trust you. You won't drop me, Seán. I'm your friend. You won't drop me.'

Seán nods once. His head is like one of those massive old bells that the lads with the ropes swing out of. Except Seán is a silent bell. He is ponderous but quiet as nightfall.

I give Seán a leg up so that he can reach the top of the wall and his runners daub my hands with mud and God alone knows what else. When he's up he lies on his belly and now I'm taking a run from halfway across the road. I'm planting one foot against the wall and I'm reaching up with my right hand. My gear bag swings awkwardly and clatters against the wall but Seán's grip is like a clamp on my forearm. The strength in him appalls me. He is a thing of awful potential, like a boulder balanced over a drop.

And then we're over the wall and into Dr Thorpe's front garden.

Dr Thorpe's house has a big huge green tongue of lawn that licks all the way up to the house, and around the back he's got so many rose bushes that when they all shed their petals at once it must be like the ground is haemorrhaging. The main driveway leads up from the gates and because it's made out of red brick all herring-boned together when we run up it we make hardly any noise at all. And as we're running I can feel my right hand tingle where Seán gripped it. I can feel my heart pumping blood into suffocated flesh.

It's when we get to the front door that things get really weird.

Seán stands with his head down again like a poor beast in the rain and I go, 'I'll do the talking.'

Seán's about to say something but he doesn't because there's a noise like a scream from inside the house.

We, me and Seán, look at each other.

Dr Thorpe's front door is a big, mahogany-red slab of wood and to either side it's got these tall skinny windows of wavy glass that reach halfway to the ground. Through them the yellow light in Dr Thorpe's hallway lights up the doorstep and the first few yards of driveway. Me and Seán stand in the yellow light and we listen hard. We don't say anything and Seán's mouth has unhinged and he's concentrating so hard that a little bit of drool is hanging from his lower lip.

We're listening so hard that the next sound makes us both jump.

Something in the house breaks and you can hear a man's voice not shouting but getting there.

Seán goes to say something but I'm putting my finger on my lips and then I'm bending down so that when I look in through the wavy glass at the side of the door I'm sort of hidden by the wooden panel at the bottom. I can't see much and the rippled glass panelling only shows shapes. Black on gold. But I'm getting a sense of perspective. I can make out the length of the hall and the bright blaze of the room at the end. It's like Dr Thorpe's house is decorated the colour of honey.

I can't see much so I bend a little lower and lift the letterbox a little. I'm lifting the letterbox and then I'm looking through.

Way down the hallway, way way down where the bright light comes from the room at the end, I can see two shapes. One on top of the other. I see Dr Thorpe and he's on top of this woman with real frizzy red hair. They are both naked and pale and sweating. He's on top of her and his hands are round her neck and they're vibrating he's squeezing so hard. Then he stops and then he's looking at her and her face isn't moving. Then something horrible happens. I'm kneeling down in the thick fake summer light of Dr Thorpe's house nearly breathing it in like breathing in the fake pine that clots the air coming through the letterbox and I'm watching Dr Thorpe do something much much worse than anything Seán's ever done. Dr Thorpe's rearing naked above the woman's own nakedness and he brings his right fist down in a long arcing missile trajectory. It smacks into her face with a hard packing sound. There's no blood yet but the woman yelps because she's been slapped back from the brink of unconsciousness. Then she gasps and grabs at her throat and looks around making this raw ragged sound, like she must have imagined what just happened.

But she isn't imagining and I'm kneeling sickened as Dr Thorpe hits her three more times. Her white limbs writhe as she kicks out beneath him. Now she's crying and wheezing and now Dr Thorpe grabs her again by the neck. There's blood coming from her lips and making jagged rivulets down her cheeks. They look like black scrawls of ink. They make her face look cracked. A cracked porcelain doll's face, broken and distorted. There's a stillness about her now. She is heavy and lax as a bag of clay. Her head has gone sideways and her eyes are looking right at me but she can't see me. She can't see anything.

She looks the way I remember my Mam looking in old photos. Like she's 2D. Like she's not really there.

I know she's dead and Dr Thorpe knows too and he leans forward and his face is so close to hers that it's like he's going to kiss her on the cheek. His talk-show host's hair is a sandy wave in the sandy light and it doesn't move and it glimmers with hairspray. His eyes have a fire in them that Seán's could never match. His eyes are shining marbles and he looks stoned. He looks ecstatic. He leans forward and he puts his finger to his lips and he says to her, 'Shhhhhhhhhh.'

I've only ever been to one proper party in my entire life and my Da hammered the shite out of me afterwards. This was last year and I'm only just gone fifteeen. This is before the fucked-up trip to Dublin and before I know what Rory's big brother does for finance. Rory, the other keeper, lives on Courthouse Street with his Ma and Da and his big brother, Davey. He lives in one of these old redbrick Edwardian houses. It's not his. His Ma and Da rent the third floor. Most of these old buildings have been chopped into segments like this. They stand along the road, rising from their little gardens. They are uniform as photocopies except that their doors are painted different colours beneath their different fanlights. Blue, yellow, green or red, they are sunk into the rust-coloured fronts of the buildings and beside each door is the grey box of a buzzer/intercom. I like these old houses. Some of their apartments are even shittier than my house.

Council Houses: Come for the space; stay for the lung infections.

Rory lives a few houses down from the old Courthouse more or less across from the Clinic and down the road from O'Leary's pub. The path along the road is always splatted with thick ropes of last night's puke and the Clinic's ground floor windows are always broken. This doesn't necessarily mean that it's a bad place to live.

What makes Rory's house a bad place to live is that a couple of weeks ago the guards break into the house's first-floor apartment. What they find is the mother of this bizarre immigrant family that lives there sitting in an armchair with her head and hands cut off. There's no sign of her husband or her children. This is plastered all over the news and the papers and Rory and his family and everyone within a half-mile radius are asked about a million questions by the guards. Rory hasn't heard a thing so he tells the guards he hasn't heard a thing. The upshot of all this is that nobody wants to live in the house except Rory and his family. Every day they tramp up the stairs and pass that locked door with the garda tape still making a big white and blue fluorescent X against the panels. Since nobody lives in the house except Rory's family, his big brother is forever throwing parties. Nobody who goes to them is put off by the garda tape and there is nobody left to complain about the noise.

It's dark and there's rain falling. The rain slants across the waspy orange of the streetlights and makes harp strings against the night. I'm wearing a jacket with the collar pulled up but even like this there's water running off my hair and down the neck of my shirt. Underneath the arches of the bridge the river is roaring and is pouring dirty white froth over the little step in the channel. A bag of cans is straining downwards from my hand and the plastic is beaded and running with rain. My jeans are a soaking navy and the bag bounces against my leg, rattling and shedding fat drops.

I'm this wet because I've walked from town down the Twenty-One Steps and then down across the river. This is a short walk in the sunlight but on a rainy night it feels like a marathon. I'm walking because I can't afford a taxi and I'm watching people who can afford taxis cruise past and I'm getting wetter and wetter. Water drips from my fringe and into my eyes and I sneeze. I am catching my death.

The headlights of the passing cars are wet-reflected and the streetlamps are suspended embers. There are three steps up to Rory's front door and in the rain they're a miniature waterfall. The buzzer beside the door is picked out in orange highlights. The dead woman's apartment has its buzzer blacked out. I'm standing in the rain and now I'm pressing Rory's buzzer and now I'm stepping back and now I'm looking up. Raindrops are hitting me in the face and are crawling down my cheeks.

The whole building is dark except for the top floor. Its windows are bright and they frame sets of cheap net curtains. Then one of the windows is opening and now Rory's leaning into the streetlight and he shouts, 'Catch!'

Next thing a big bunch of keys comes tumbling and chiming

down through the rain. I'm standing here waiting for the keys to fall and I'm wondering how did Rory recognise me from up there in the dark? Not that it matters. The keys are falling at a velocity of thirty feet per second from a height of roughly forty feet. When they hit my cold, wet hand it hurts like someone's hit it with a hammer but I don't want to risk losing them in the dark so my sore hand spasms closed around them and their chiming goes dead.

I eventually find the right key and the interior of Rory's house is black dark except for the stairwell. I know there's the ceramic nipple of an old-fashioned light switch sticking out from the wall by the door but I don't use it. The light coming down the stairs is kind of hazy and weak but it's enough to find your way up. Rory's flat is on the top floor and first you've to climb to two landings. The stairs and landings are fleeced with grey carpet and on the first landing you've to walk past the blue and white fluorescent X of crime scene tape. I don't look at it.

The door to Rory's flat is open a crack. Out of it comes a yelping overlay of conversation. It sounds like a dog kennel. You climb the grey stairs which you don't pay attention to and you go past the garda tape which you make sure you don't pay attention to and now you're at this half-open door. It's a gap into someplace warm and vital. So what do you do? I stand there for a moment listening to the noise of conversation and I drip quietly, a soft patpatpat onto the carpet.

Then someone goes, 'Would you come in for fuck's sake. You're letting in a draught.'

How do you refuse an invitation like that?

I'm pushing open the door and then I'm through into Rory's flat and I'm shutting the door behind me. The place is thick with warmth but I'm shivering because the water that's soaked into me is like ice in this atmosphere. Now I'm dropping the bag of cans and now I'm massaging some life back into my rainslicked fingers. Then I'm sneezing. I've definitely caught something.

Rory's house is pretty big. It consists of a sitting room/kitchen and three bedrooms. I'm standing in the sitting room/kitchen and as far as the eye can see the floor is a bristle of candles. Each one is lit and each bouquet of wax is crowned with a blossom of fire. This explains the heat. What explains the thick, acrid smell of hash is the fact that all twelve people in the room are well on the road to being stoned. They sit or stand in twos or threes and they're all engaged in guffawing conversation. Four guitars are leaning against one wall. Because anyone can play guitar.

Rory comes from around the jutting wall that divides the smoky humidity of the sitting room from the smoky humidity of the kitchen. I'm standing like a drowning man held upright by rigor mortis and Rory goes, 'Jaysus, is it raining?'

I go, 'This is sweat.'

Now Rory's coming towards me carrying a can in one hand and a sausage sandwich in the other. Brown sauce is leaking between his fingers in fat tongues. Brown sauce is making a ring around his mouth and he's saying, 'Ah you're a funny fucker. Grab a can or something and sit down, you're making the place look untidy.' Then he's taking a bite from his sandwich and then he's walking over to two lads trying to get a bong going in a corner. I'm standing there with my jacket soaked and heavy and my jeans glued to the scrawny knots of my knees. The brown carpet beneath my bag of cans is sodden and it is three shades too dark.

I don't know anyone here yet so I'm lifting the bag of cans and now I'm putting them into the fridge and now I'm coming back from the kitchen with a can of Dutchie in my hand. My hair and jeans are still saturated but my jacket is now off and hanging on a kitchen chair to dry. I'm still cold and shivering, though.

There are three armchairs and a couch making an upholstered semicircle around a coffee table in the centre of the room. There's a very very attractive girl sitting on the couch next to another not-so-attractive girl. I'm thinking of going over to sit beside her but then she's looking me and her eyes are taking in my plastered hair and drenched jeans and then her upper lip curls and her eyes look away. I'm thinking that I don't want to sit beside her after all. This is my first real party and I'm feeling pretty nervous. Most of the people here are way older than me and Rory. They're all his brother's friends from college. I've never liked Rory's brother. I know everyone says how he's the biggest dealer in the town. Everyone says how the guards are just waiting to get Davey on something big. But he's not here. Not beside the very very attractive girl. Not smoking with the others. Not anywhere. This is a good thing. In spite of the very very attractive girl's venomous appraisal of me, I'm smiling.

I'm smiling and now I'm sitting with my back to a wall. I think I'm starting to dry out and the beer tastes good. I'm sitting beside a bunch of candles and the heat radiating off them is beginning to seep into my flesh. It's a welcome relief from getting pissed on. Most of the candles standing around the place are set on plates or saucers but some genius, probably Rory, has set a good few on old CDs. The CDs are title-side down so that the candles are planted in the mounds of wax accumulating on the silvered sides. A band of rainbow colour makes a bright radius from the base of each candle to the outer edge of each CD. The discs look like puddles of glowing mercury. What whoever set the candles on them fails to realise is that if the candles are let burn down, the nice puddles of mercury will turn into small infernos.

People are arriving now in small groups. I'm the only one who turned up here on my own. Don't get me wrong, I'm not some wild-eyed recluse. I'm chatting to people and having a laugh with everyone except the very very attractive girl. I think we got off on the wrong foot. I'm not too distressed over this fact, nor am I over the fact that I arrived here on my own. Neither am I suicidal over the fact that I'll probably be leaving on my own as well. Ninety-nine times out of a hundred I leave even teenage discos on my own. I'm used to it. I'm moving about the place and the smoke is getting thicker and everyone's starting to get a bit louder. Now I'm talking to two lads from my football team and now I'm listening to them bitch about a teacher they both have. Everyone else laughs and smokes and drinks.

Rory's brother's friends all seem to be stuck in the sixties. They are all hippies. It is only a matter of time before one of them picks up a guitar and starts playing Joni Mitchell or Van Morrison.

Dead Dogs

I'm thinking this and then someone's doing this.

He is a thin guy with an earnest face. His eyes are bloodshot from smoking and seem cut-and-pasted from Droopy Dog. He's picking up a guitar and then he's playing the first few chords of 'Big Yellow Taxi'. It's more Counting Crows than Joni Mitchell but no one seems to mind. The guy playing the guitar sings with his eyes shut. It's like he's in pain. He keeps time by tapping the beat out on the floor with a pair of hundred-and-twenty quid runners. The two lads from the football team are now dancing with each other.

Now the other guitars have joined in and the music is stuck somewhere between the late sixties and early seventies. Someone's starting to play a Christie Moore tune and then I'm getting a beer and then I'm bumping into Davey.

This happens because I'm coming back from the kitchen and I'm checking my phone for messages. I'm walking with my head down and I'm walking with my mind elsewhere and I'm walking straight into Davey's chest.

He goes, 'You'd really want to watch where you're going'.

I'm looking at him and I'm trying to say something and then I'm sneezing again.

The rest of the party suddenly feels about a million miles away and Davey's saying, 'Bless you.'

The party has now left our solar system and its fake hippy, faux-folk strumming is receding into the background like the smell of air freshener. It's like myself and Davey are at the centre of a rapidly expanding circle of empty space. But not one person moves away from us. The party's Brownian motion continues and the very very attractive girl is brushing past Davey and at the same time everyone's leaving orbit.

I'm feeling this and I'm looking at Davey and I'm thinking, ground control to Major Tom I think we have a problem.

From the centre of our total exclusion zone, from the centre of our private vacuum, I'm saying, 'Good party.' My words are clear and perfectly discernible through the cords of smoke and over the sound of Luca who lives on the second floor of some other house in some other galaxy.

Davey takes this with what I'm beginning to realise is a non-chalance born of arrogance. He's looking at me like I've just told a joke. His shoulders are wet from the rain where it's soaked through whatever jacket he was wearing and his hair is dripping. There's some kind of wax or gel in it, so the water's gathered on it like blisters and where the light hits it it throws off blue high-lights. Like Superman.

He is smiling and for a second I'm thinking maybe I have told a joke.

Then he goes, 'You don't mean that. If you want to be invited to all the best shindigs, I'd suggest you work on your sincerity, little man.'

Then he's walking around me on the way to the kitchen and now the party comes crashing back on top of me. It is the Big Bang in reverse. It is a falling anvil.

All of Rory's brother's friends are Arts students. All of Rory's brother's friends are now drunk. The music is all done except for two girls who are both trying to play the same guitar. One girl is making the chords while the other tries to strum. They are both fucking up royally. The one doing the strumming has lost all coordination and she keeps tangling the plectrum in the middle strings. The one making the chords is slightly more together but every so often a string doesn't ring true and it buzzes like a fridge, like a detuned radio. They're attempting to play a Radiohead song. The one girl's terrible strumming is attracting slagging from her friend and the comments are getting more and more sarcastic and more and more cutting. You can tell from strummer girl's face that it won't be long before she's bleeding tears.

I'm watching them from where I'm sitting on a chair dragged from the kitchen. The can in my hand is almost empty but I'm not sure if I can get another because the floor to the kitchen is paved with comatose people. There's a cumulous cushion of smoke clinging to the ceiling. It is the colour of dishwater.

I don't smoke but my eyes are red and heavy from the atmosphere and now they're closing and opening again like in slow motion. Davey does smoke but he's watching me from the couch with eyes like polished black stones. He is wide awake. He's watching me and then he's curling his fingers in the blonde hair of the very very attractive girl and then he's grinning at me. The girl is listing into his side and upon her neck is the ripe plum mark of his lips and teeth.

We don't say anything and I'm watching him watching me like through someone else's eyes.

I'm drunk and I'm tired and he's more alive than ever. I'm thinking something about vampires and then I'm falling asleep.

And then I'm waking up because the nearly empty can I'm holding isn't so empty that I don't feel it slipping out of my hand. Everything is natural now. No day-glo chords to highlight emotion. No chatter to clutter the night. There is only the sound of breathing, heavy and sleep-drugged and tidal.

I don't know why but I can hear dead leaves in the wind.

This is what's going through my head as I'm waking. Then I'm wondering, can I smell burning? Then I'm thinking, fuck, I can smell burning. Now I'm opening my eyes and now I'm looking around. This is easier said than done because I have the beginnings of a hangover and it feels like something's died in my mouth. My eyes are filmed with sandpaper but I'm taking in the difference in the smoke. I'm taking in the small black flakes yawing through the air, I'm taking in Davey standing up and looking at something. And now I'm taking in the fire.

The candles set on the CDs have burned down to nothing and now they've set the CDs on fire which have in turn set the wallpaper on fire. The flames are scuttling halfway up the wall by now and the surrounding wallpaper is beginning to peel and blacken. Like dead leaves in the wind. The ceiling is smoke-smudged and I'm thinking Rory must not have a fire alarm. Everyone except me and Davey is asleep. This is not a good thing.

I'm about to scream, I'm about to yell, I'm about to raise the roof and then Davey's putting a finger to his lips and he goes, 'Shhhhhhhhhh.'

My tongue turns to clay and I'm sitting watching him watching the fire and I can't do anything. I don't know why this is. I am a vegetable. I am an empty void.

I don't know how long I sit silently with Davey watching the fire climb the wall, watching the smoke make a black rose upon the white ceiling. I don't know how long I sit watching Davey watching the melted CDs eat into the carpet like a cancer. I don't know how long it is until the very very attractive girl starts to stir. Then she's coughing in her sleep, coughing in little rattling barks.

Then Davey's moving. He's picking up two nearly full cans and now he's pouring them down the wall and now I'm yelling, 'Fire!' and now I'm screaming, 'Fire!' like a fucking broken record. Davey's pouring more beer to drown the fire and now he's using someone's jacket to smother the burning CDs. I'm watching Davey do this and then I'm on my feet and helping him.

I'm angry at myself for sitting there so long. I'm angry at myself for letting Davey play out this little charade. I'm angry at myself for being shushed and staying shushed. Davey's grinning again and he winks at me through the smoke. In spite of my anger my mouth grins back.

Everyone else is awake now. They're getting up from the floor like extras in a zombie movie. They are all stiff-limbed and loose-faced. Most of them are wide-eyed with terror. You can see the whites of their eyes the whole way around and now they remind me of frightened horses. Through all this Davey is still grinning and the fire's almost out and for the first time in my life I see something terrifying behind the smoke of the everyday. In

Davey's face I see a man ready to watch the whole lot go up in flames.

I'm looking around at the terrified tottering things that are Rory's friends. They look shocked and I'm standing with my hands sooty and chest heaving and I'm apart from them. Not just apart but above. Their still-stoned, still-drunk eyes blink at me like those of slaughterhouse animals, dim-witted and blankly grateful. I'm thinking this and then I'm thinking, what if they had burned? What difference would it have made? Would their absence be filled by someone else? I'm thinking this and then Rory's pumping my hand.

He's still drunk as a lord and his voice has the consistency of porridge. He's coughing a bit because of the smoke and the reek of the burning. Then he's going, 'Fucking hell, son! Jesus Christ! Thanks, thanks, thanks. Christ, we all could've been killed!'

But all I can hear is Davey's sea-surge 'Shhhhhhhhhh,' and the light in his eyes as he watches the flames.

This is how Dr Thorpe looks. It is the same eagerness, the same rapture, the same light. It is the expression of a man watching something burn to ashes and revelling in it.

And then I'm blinking and then I'm falling away from the glass and the letterbox, falling so hard that I land on my arse in the middle of the doorstep. I'm sitting on my arse in the middle of the doorstep and Seán is looking at me like I'm something from a different planet.

I'm scrambling to my feet and I'm hoping to God that I haven't made much of a noise. Seán is looking confused and now he's moving over to the golden slot of the still-open letterbox.

I grab him by the arm and I go, 'Don't look, Seán. We have to get the fuck out of here.'

Then, quieter, I'm going, 'We'll get you sorted somewhere else.'

Seán's frowning at me and he's whispering in this stage whisper like he thinks this is how you're supposed keep your voice down. He's saying, 'But I like Dr Thorpe. He's nice.'

I look from Seán to the red slab of mahogany door with its carved panels and tasteful lacquer. I look from Seán to the door and then back and I'm remembering the sound that Dr Thorpe's fist makes as it connects with the poor woman's face. The dead meat smack of it. I look from Seán to the door and then I go, 'Dr Thorpe's not a nice man, Seán. There's no way he's a nice man.'

Seán blinks at me slowly like the way elephants blink, calm and placid and with all the time in the world.

My voice is this slithering whispering thing because I'm terrified that Dr Thorpe will come out and find us and I'm saying in this slithering whispering voice, 'Are you sure you haven't got your phone?'

Seán nods and I go, 'Fuck it.'

I go, 'We have to get out of here. I'll tell you why when we're over that wall.'

Seán's staring at the door now and his face is in flux. He knows I've seen something and he knows that it's frightened the bejeezus out of me. He's like a hunting dog set on some scent that compels and repels him at the same time. Still staring at the door he goes, 'I don't like it here. I want to go home. I told you I wanted to go home.'

I honestly don't know what to do. I know we have to tell the guards but then we'd have to explain how we got here. We'd have to explain about Seán's dead dogs. My stomach feels like a swinging bag filled with acid.

I saying, 'We'll go to my house. I have to tell my Da. And you're coming with me.'

A minute later I'm hanging down the outside of Dr Thorpe's wall, holding on by my fingertips. The lip of the concrete is jagged and splintered into broken little saw-edges. I can feel the concrete digging into my hands and I know that if I don't let go all in one go the stuff will just gouge red-leaking furrows in my skin. Wet concrete is horrible to the touch. It's all cold and clammy and it feels the way you'd think a chest infection would feel if you could touch a chest infection.

Seán's already on the path underneath and he goes, 'I'll catch you.' Then he's reaching up and his hands are all cupped like he's about to catch a ball and they are about six inches away from my butt cheeks.

In spite of everything, in spite of the dog and her pups lying in the mess of their own dying, in spite of seeing Dr Thorpe do what he did, in spite of all this, I go, 'Seán, if you touch my arse, I'll box the fucking forehead off you.'

Seán takes his hands away and I drop to the ground. My

hands are cold and sore from hanging onto the wall but they're not cut, not weeping blood. I'm strangely thankful for this and it's like my hands not being shredded is the best thing that's happened all evening.

Right down from where I live there's a shop beside the bus stop. There's a shop beside the bus stop and usually outside it there's a guy with a South Dublin accent and a Lacoste shirt talking into a mobile phone. When you get off the bus you'd swear it was someone off a TV3 lifestyle show. Same clothes. Same hairstyle. Same fucking accent. Everything. These guys are usually accompanied by their girlfriends or mates and they're usually catching the bus back to Dublin from *Weckie*. I kid you not.

The first thing you notice when you get off the bus is the New Bridge. It is the colour of doves' feathers and it makes a flat trajectory across the river. If you're halfway across the New Bridge you can see that the castle and the spires of the twin cathedrals are black spikes against the sky. From my house, you cross the New Bridge, go up Castle Hill, swing right through the Market Square, walk up past the Cathedral, down past the Fair Green and the primary school and you're more or less at Dr Thorpe's.

If you were heading from my house to Dr Thorpe's right now you'd meet me and Seán coming the other way. Me and Seán are now half-walking half-jogging past the big, green-painted, steel gates of the primary school. I'm going to Seán, 'Don't draw any attention. Keep calm.'

Seán looks as calm as a doldrum sea and I'm saying these words in a sort of chant. They are a mantra to keep me from breaking into a freaked-out run. I'm the on the very verge of panic.

Seán keeps pace with me as we go from orange to black to orange beneath the streetlights and he goes, 'What about the dead dogs? What about my tablets? Why are we running away? What did you see through the letterbox?'

He's asking these questions and he's looking at me with his great, dull cinders for eyes.

My breath is coming too quickly and my tongue feels like a wet cotton rag but I know that Seán needs to be told something so I say, 'We'll get tablets from another doctor, Seán. We won't tell anyone about the dead dogs but we have to tell my Da about what I saw Dr Thorpe do.'

I'm looking at Seán's blunt profile now and he's not even out of breath. He trots along beside me like he could keep this up all night. I'm swallowing and then I'm going, 'Dr Thorpe is a bad man. I saw him do something bad to a woman.'

Seán takes this in like still waters swallowing a carcass and he goes, 'Did he rape her or hit her or something?'

I say, 'I don't know if he raped her but he definitely hit her.'

Take a pack of rashers and slide all that wet, slimy dead pig out of the plastic. Then drop the rashers onto a cold, hard floor. This is the sound that Dr Thorpe's fist makes.

Seán goes, 'Oh.' He accepts everything I say without any sort of question. He says this with calm, with equipoise. The emotion he shows is curiosity, not horror, and he goes, 'He shouldn't do things like that.'

And in that tone I hear everything that's wrong with Seán Galvin.

We're heading down through the Square now with its steps and its statue put up to commemorate 1798. The big bronze priest is pointing off toward Vinegar Hill and the croppy boy is all noble-faced and proud in the daylight. Now, though, with the streetlamps greasing him with their light, the croppy boy has this strange expression. There's a certain fall of shadow and a certain quirk of lighting that makes it look like the croppy boy, with his pike and farmer's shirt, the croppy boy with his slash-hook for a sword, is thinking, *Are you taking the piss, Father?*

Now we're jogging down past the Castle and now we're on the New Bridge. The water is sliding beneath us and now I'm stopping and now I'm cursing and now Seán's going, 'What's wrong?'

I'm staring back the way we came and the town mounts the slope and climbs away from me. The roofs and chimneys step away toward the weeping dark of the horizon except you can't see the horizon. There's just more roofs and more chimneys and then when you get to the edge of town there's the mountains sitting in the distance like big blue anvils. You can never see far around here. Lines of sight are never true and perspective gets lost real easy.

In my mind's eye I'm looking back the way we came and I'm seeing Dr Thorpe's driveway and then I'm seeing Dr Thorpe's front porch. And there, right in the middle so that if you open the door you can't help but trip over the fucking thing, I'm seeing my gear bag. My name screams out from the bag's red fabric panelling in heavy, black permanent marker.

Just like that the world is falling away from me and it's like I'm occupying a bubble of air suspended way above anything. I'm suddenly really really cold and I feel like I'm going to vomit again and that my bowels are going to let go all at the same time.

Again Seán goes, 'What's wrong?'

And I go, 'I left my bag on the doorstep. It has my name on it.'

And Seán says, 'Shite.'

I take a step back the way we came but then I stop and then I look at Seán and then I go, 'We can't go back.'

Seán nods placidly and he says, 'Are we in trouble? I told you we'd get in trouble. Are we?'

Above the burbling noise that's coming from my guts, I go, 'I think so. Yeah.'

When you cross the New Bridge my house is up the hill on the right. There used to be a factory there but it was demolished and eight new Council Houses were built over its bones. I don't think you're supposed to call them *Council Houses* anymore. Instead, you're supposed to call them *Affordable Housing*. *Affordable Housing* or *Social Housing*. It all means the same thing. It all means you can't afford to buy a house of your own so you get stuck with what the Council gives you. Da doesn't like this pointed out to him.

My front door looks nothing like Dr Thorpe's. It's a big rectangle of veneer tacked over nothing but empty space with another piece of veneer tacked onto its back. You'd put your fist through it if you really wanted. Dermot Sinnott, three doors down, did just that a couple of days ago. There's no reasoning with Dermot when he has a few jars in him and his wife is always wandering around explaining to people how she can't stop falling down the stairs.

When I turn my key in the lock and open the front door my Da is standing there in the hall. Before I can say how glad I am to see him, before I can say that I think I've witnessed a murder, before I can even open my mouth he's saying stuff.

He's saying, 'Why don't you ever bring your phone with you?'

And then he's saying, 'I just got a phonecall from Dr Thorpe. He wants to speak with you.'

Mam and me and Da, we all used to live out on the Still Road. This shitty little house on a loop of the road, huddled under the Turret Rocks, is not where I grew up. I'm too young to know how this happened and Da never says but I think Mam's medical bills were pretty high and I think when Da lost his job out in the factory a couple of years ago he couldn't keep up the payments and lost the house. That's a lot of losses all at the one time.

A couple of years ago when I still live out by the Still it's the third week of the summer holidays. We have three months off from the first week in June to the last week in August and for the next while life at home is one long yawn. Da gets up and puts on his overalls and heads to work. My aunt, Da's sister, does the shopping. I sleep in. Things start to slide a bit when my aunt goes to pay with Da's Laser card and it won't go through. She asks Da where all the money's gone. She asks Da what he's done with his wages. Da blinks like a toddler, gormless and hurt, and says he doesn't know. My aunt spends the next week ringing banks and tax offices and Da gets up, puts on his overalls and heads to work.

I'm tired of sleeping in. Eleven o'clock in the morning and I pull open the curtains and I'm standing in my boxers looking out at the sun on our road, standing in my boxers looking out at a blue tarpaulin sky. In the brightness my body looks made out of candle wax. I don't like this. I don't like missing half the day. I am a morning person.

A lot of days during the summer I get up and I shower and I walk down to the Banks. The Banks are just that. The banks of the Slaney river in town. They are flat and grassy and paved only with chippings. People from town walk along the Banks a lot, not like the Prom where you get the people staying in the hotel saun-tering along cooing at the river over the dull hiss of the N11. I like this walk along the Banks because it takes a long while and you can think a lot when you're doing it. I sometimes write stories and I like to think about where they're going when I don't have to think about where I'm going.

To get down to the Banks you're walking away from town and cars and people go by you in the opposite direction. Some of them have questioning expressions on their faces. A young boy in a tracksuit bottoms and T-shirt on his own and moving against the tide. One or two say good morning. Genuinely genuine women in genuine Dunnes tracksuits being genuinely friendly. Going to school in a place where there's over a thousand other kids just like you desensitizes you to indifference. It desensitises you so much that you greet these comments like they're door-to-door salesmen in cheap polyester crackling with static.

I like this stroll. This pushing against a stream that doesn't push back. I like the Banks. You strip the surface from a tree and it's still a tree. A river is still a river. Everything is as it seems. The sun on the Slaney's red wave makes me smile. A genuinely genuine smile.

Standing looking out my window it is eleven o'clock in the morning and I decide to go for a stroll.

The easiest way to get to the Banks from my house is to go down to the bottom of the road through the Council estate, go down Nunnery Lane and cross the Dublin Road. Nunnery Lane's not even a lane. It's a beaten track of grass and dirt zigging between briars and zagging between the mesh fence of the primary school. In the summer the briars and blackthorns are spattered with blossoms and insects are a white noise in the grass. In the winter though the place is dead and the path is so greasy it's like it's floored with eels.

But in the summer, like it is now, it makes the perfect shortcut.

I'm halfway down Nunnery Lane and I'm listening to the grass and lashes of briar are snagging and catching on my tracksuit. I'm thinking how there wasn't any food in the fridge today. And now I'm wondering if everything's alright with Da and his sister. I'm wondering this and I'm walking along and a briar hooks my hand and tears a little red crescent in the web of skin between thumb and forefinger. On a branch just as you come to the road there's the drooping amniotic sac of a condom. I don't know who impaled it there on the thorns but there's stuff in it and I don't touch it as I go by.

The path down to the Banks is covered in gravel. The gravel is all steel-coloured chippings and I'm listening to it grind under my feet and I can feel its hard angles through the soles of my runners. The river is on my right and it gurgles along shallow and looking like chocolate in the heat. Across the water the flat meadow of the Island is spangled with geysers of wildflowers and horses in a swirl of flies are cropping the plants. The ground on my left slopes up and up to the road and slopes up and up covered in trees.

When you're walking along like this you can see along the river and you can look over your shoulder to see the town built along both sides of the valley. From where I am, I can see fields and cows and the black fleck of a person in the distance. The person isn't moving, they're just standing there in the distance where the cows have trampled a pitted slipway down to the river. The blades of mud between the hoofprints will be made hard as terracotta by the sun. And in the distance the black fleck just stands there and I keep walking.

I keep walking and now I'm thinking how shrill my aunt sounded when she was asking Da about the money. Not accusing but getting there.

And for the last while since, every day, Da goes to work. He gets up puts on his overalls and goes to work.

There are an awful lot of weeds coming up through the gravel. The farther you go away from the Dublin road the more grass and dandelions there are. Every time I step on one, every time I step on a dandelion, my runners crush it flat. It stays there pressed against the gravel bleeding its white milk blood. There's a stile between the path and this big field that runs along the river for a couple of hundred yards. The stile makes a hole in a fence of barbed wire. The gravel rattles up to this stile and then stops dead. It doesn't continue into the field but the path does. It is a worn track of bare earth. At least once a day, seven days a week, three hundred and sixty five days a year, someone walks along here. It's gotten so that if you get right down you can see the effects of all this weight. It's gotten so that on your hands and knees you can see the trench that the path is becoming. Once a day, seven days a week, three hundred and sixty five days a year, is starting to make the riverbank subside.

I'm standing at this stile and now the black fleck up ahead is starting to look like a man. I'm standing at this stile and now my face is starting to make a weird expression. I know this because I can feel the muscles of my jaw spasm and I can feel my lower lip twitch and I can feel my eyes go wider and wider. It's like they're trying to suck in and swallow everything in front of them.

I'm standing here with one foot on the gravel and one foot on the stile and my face is looking like melting plastic because I recognise the man on the riverbank.

I recognise him because he's my Da.

The next day my Da tells my aunt that he's been let go. But he doesn't tell her since when. He never says for how long he got up, put on his overalls and went to a work that doesn't exist.

He never says why he gets let go. He never says what happened. What really happened.

This is my Da. He won't ever, ever meet a problem head-on.

I'm listening to my Da saying that Dr Thorpe wants to speak with me and I can feel Seán tense up behind me. I'm listening to my Da saying this and what I'm thinking is, Da's going to be fucking useless in this situation.

He's standing in the hallway and his hands are all knotted together into white balls of gristle so that it's like he's praying really hard for something. He's lost most of his hair and the forty-watt bulb hanging above him is slicking his pate with a light that looks jaundiced. He doesn't look healthy and his face is a shifting swamp of worry.

He's going, 'What have you done, boys? Seán, are you in trouble?'

All the time he blames Seán for stuff. No matter what I get myself into, he blames Seán.

My shitty results in maths? Seán.

See also my superhuman ability to repel girls.

See also my problems with some of the other lads from around town.

Everything is Seán's fault.

My Da refuses to allow me to take responsibilty for anything. It's like I'm a miniature version of himself. You just avoid things or yoke them onto someone else or hide yourself under the covers until they go away. If life fucks you over, you just put on your overalls and keep leaving the house like everything's all A-okay. You live in the vain hope that things will somehow turn out fine. That there's been some big mistake somewhere. That the universe is sorry for throwing sand in your face. Anything other than confront the fact that you may have to actually *do* something.

This is what yer man from *Teens in the Wild* calls *avoidance*. It follows from a lack of self-esteem. Like everything else in the entire fucking world. I hate psychology. It is snake-oil and make-believe.

I hate psychology because Seán's gone to about a zillion psychologists and he's still all screwy in the head.

I'm looking at my Da and I'm watching him wring his hands and I'm saying, 'Seán didn't do anything.'

This isn't strictly true, but I figure I have bigger fish to fry at the moment.

Seán goes to say something but I hit him an elbow and Da's seeing me doing this but I keep going anyway. I'm saying, 'I think I've seen something that's going to sound really weird but I swear to God it's all true.'

Da's looking at me and he's frowning and behind me and Seán the front door swings closed.

Da listens to me as I blurt out what happened at Dr Thorpe's. I tell him what I saw through the letterbox. What I heard. The dead meat smack of it.

And Da goes, 'Why were you at Dr Thorpe's?'

No outraged squawking that his sixteen-year-old son may have just witnessed a murder. No scrambling for the phone to tell the guards. Just an accusatory question. The pedictable fucking supposition that we were up to no good.

I go, 'Jesus, Da. Are you not listening? Never mind why we were there. You have to go to the guards or something. They'll believe you. You're a grown-up.'

We're having this conversation in the hallway and the light from the dim bulb is staining everything like with tannin and the chipboard wallpaper on the narrow walls seems to be about to peel off and smother me. The smell of the mince and onions that Da's fried for dinner is making me sick.

Da looks from me to Seán and back again and then he's going, 'This is Seán's fault, isn't it? Why else would you be at the doctor's? Well, I'll tell you this, my fine lads, if you're going to go around making up stories about people to cover your own arses then I'm not going to help you.'

Seán's starting to groan and I go, 'Da, you're being stupid. We told you because if the guards knew Seán was involved there's no way they'd believe us. They'd start asking questions and stuff. You're my Da. You have to believe me.'

Da's frowning now and he's scratching his jaw and he's saying, 'I don't have to believe anything. We're all going to go to Dr Thorpe's and we'll hear what he has to say. Hopefully he won't be too pissed off that you two were sneaking around his garden like peeping fucking Toms.'

He goes to Seán, 'And stop that fucking moaning, Seán Galvin.

Ring your Da and tell him where we're going. You better pray to Jesus that he doesn't beat the the shite out of you when you get home.'

Then he wrinkles his nose and he goes, 'What's that smell?'

Before Seán can say anything I go, 'Seán hasn't got his phone on him.'

And Seán says, 'Da took it until I cop myself on.'

Da looks at us like we're that sort of gunk you get in the bottom of a bin and he goes, 'Jesus Christ. What are you two like? Use the house phone.'

Seán goes past my Da and into our kitchen. Da goes, 'I need a slash.' And then he's muttering something and then he's heading upstairs.

I wait until I hear the bathroom door closing and then I go into the kitchen after Seán. Our kitchen is all lino and woodchip and the air is gritty with the smells of frying. Seán is talking into the phone that we have screwed to one wall. It's bright candy red and looks like a slightly more modern version of the Batphone that Commissioner Gordon has in his office.

Seán's saying, 'No, Da.'

Then he's saying, 'Yes, Da.'

From down the phone line and from out of the earpiece I can hear a dry leaf voice say something short and sharp and now Seán's sighing and he goes, 'I promise, Da.'

Seán hangs up and before he has a chance to say anything to me I'm grapping the receiver off him and I'm dialling the number for the guards' barracks. Seán's looking at me with that strange empty expression that he gets when he doesn't know what's going on. I put my fingers to my lips to tell him to be quiet and then a voice in this real thick midlands accent starts talking out of the phone.

I'm thinking I recognise the voice and it goes, 'Hello. Garda Station.'

I'm swallowing like my throat is filled with wet rags and I don't know what to say and the guard at the other end of the line says, 'Hello? Can you hear me?'

Before the guard gets annoyed and hangs up I go, 'I think I've seen someone commit a murder.'

The guard splutters down the phone and I can picture his coffee and his copy of the *Sun* being knocked off his desk. I can picture the Page Three girl grinning up at him from the floor.

And now this spluttering, panicked guard, he's going, 'Can I have your name, sir. Your name and the details of what you've seen.'

Down the phone I just go, 'Dr Thorpe's on the Nunnery Road. You have to get there quick.'

Then I hang up.

From up the stairs I can hear the toilet flush, the bathroom door unlock and the shuffling plod of my Da as he comes back down the stairs. When he comes into the kitchen he looks at me and Seán and he looks at the swinging umbilical cord of the phone. He looks at all this and me and Seán must look pretty suspicious because he goes, 'What are you two up to?'

And like we've rehearsed it me and Seán go, 'Nothing,' at the exact same time.

Da has a jacket in his hand and he slings it on over his shoulders and zips up the front. He's still looking at us suspiciously and his eyes are little slivers of bright glass under his frown and he says to Seán, 'Did you ring your Da?'

Seán nods quickly like he has a twitch or something.

Da goes, 'What did he say?'

Seán looks at the lino and he's going, 'He says I'm going to get a kick in the hole when I get home.'

Da grunts a horrible little snort of satisfaction at this and then he goes to herd me and Seán out into the hall.

He's doing this and I'm saying, 'Da, we can't go to Dr Thorpe's. He's after killing someone. I saw him. Why don't you believe me?'

Da's behind me now and he's shoving me in front of him like a snowplough nosing along a dirty ball of slush. He's looking at me trying to face him over my shoulder and he says, 'Don't be stupid. After all the trouble he's gotten you into lately, you expect me to believe a cock-and-bull story like that? Give me a break. If you've done any damage to Dr Thorpe's roses you'll work your arse off to make up for it.'

Seán's hurrying along in front of us. He looks at me with his wide, flat eyes and I can see my own fear reflected in them.

Da's shoving me in the back and he's going, 'Not another word out of you.'

Since Da lost his job we've had to cut back on stuff. He hardly ever goes out anymore and he does most of the shopping in what he calls *Poundshops*. When I was little Mam and Da used to get me packets of green plastic soldiers and cap guns out of these shops. Now Da gets our toilet roll and shower gel, our toothpaste and our washing up liquid. One of the other things that happened when Da lost his job was that he couldn't afford the car. So he sold it. We walk everywhere now and if we want to go to Wexford or Dublin we get the bus or the train.

Because we don't have a car, Da's marching us step by step back the way we came. We go down the hill and cross the concrete slab of the New Bridge and then up past the Castle. The Castle's windows are these rectangular, white, double-glazed things so out of keeping with the streaming green of the old stonework that it's almost obscene. The windows are wet-slick in the light from the street and because they're elongated and the rooms beyond are black-dark they look mournful. Like the building is crying. We're past the Castle and into the Market Square and then we head on up past the towering spike of the Cathedral.

With every step I'm more and more afraid and I can hear Seán start to make his moaning noise but really low down in his chest so that the sound is more a vibration. It's as if fear and confusion are radiating off him like static.

A couple of times I try and talk to my Da but every time he says, 'I've had enough out of you. That's enough.'

And once, hard and bitter like his voice was something squeezed from a crab apple, he goes, 'As if we haven't gone through enough without you sneaking around people's gardens.'

Dr Thorpe's isn't the same as when we left it. For a start, the heavy black gates are open and they sit unmoving and cold at the end of the long, curved grooves they've scarred into the brickwork of Dr Thorpe's driveway. Another thing that's different is that there's a squad car parked at the top of the drive and Dr Thorpe's front door is open. The light from his house makes a bright puddle of his porch and in the light I can see Dr Thorpe with his fused crest of hair, and standing in front of him is the big blue-black silhouette of a guard in full uniform, shirt and stab vest and hat. Against the light the guard is nodding at something Dr Thorpe is saying.

Da pulls up short when he sees the squad car and the guard and he grabs me by the collar and he goes, 'Did you ring the guards? You did, didn't you? That's what the two of you were doing in the kitchen looking like butter wouldn't melt in your mouths.'

He looks at the guard and at me and then he looks at Seán and he goes, 'What in God's name did you do that for? They'll have you for trespass or something. Fuck's sake.'

He starts to walk up the driveway way quicker than he should. He's not quite running but it looks like he wants to so that it's like he's doing that speed walking thing from the Olympics. It's the most inelegant thing in the world. This would be funny except for the fact that he's jabbing me in front of him and Seán's following along behind like a stray puppy.

My runners are scuffing off the brickwork and in my chest my heart is palpitating like it's in spasm. The guards being here is the best thing that's happened since this crazy fucking evening began. I'm thinking, Dr Thorpe's fucked now. There's no way he's had a chance to hide the body. I'm thinking the guard will want to do a search or take him down to the barracks for questioning. I'm picturing the interview room, featureless and washed-out, all drab and shaded in grey and old bone. I'm picturing Dr Thorpe being grilled by Bunk and McNulty out of *The Wire*.

I'm thinking, Da will have to believe me now.

And then the guard is turning around to face us and then what I'm thinking is, For fuck's sake.

This guard with his slab head, his shovels for hands and a meaty roll of flesh like a sausage sitting just above the collar of his shirt. This guard with his thin, joyless mouth, I recognise him.

We're close enough now so that I can see that Dr Thorpe is smiling, and he goes, 'Ah, here they are now.'

This all happens just before Seán gets put on his little red tablets. His little red *useless* tablets. This is the first time I meet this guard that a few months later is standing with Dr Thorpe when he says, 'Ah, here they are now.'

When I get home from training one night this same guard's sitting in the kitchen drinking coffee. He's sitting at the table and his uniform is dark in the light and his hat is resting on the counter behind him. His hands are curled around the mug in front of him like he's trying to warm himself up and between the knuckles of his right hand ceramic letters can be read. They don't make sense fractured and broken like they are now but I know that under the guard's hands are the words *I like my job, it's the work I hate.*

I'm looking at this guard and then I'm wondering, what have I done? My head is spooling through every little thing that might have caused this. Looking at him with his big hands gripping the mug I'm thinking, it has to be the porn I was looking up on the computer. I'm thinking it's pretty fucked up that typing *huge jugs* into Google can land a guard at your kitchen table.

My Da is standing behind the guard and he's white white white except for his cheeks. They are haemorrhage red and make it look like he's wearing Aunt Sally's make-up. Between his hands a dishcloth is knotting and twisting and unknotting again. His hands are manic and his knuckles are the same white white white as his face. He's mouthing something at me over the guard's head but I can't understand him. I'm standing in the kitchen doorway and I'm staring over his head and the guard goes, 'If you wouldn't mind giving us a little privacy, Jack.'

He doesn't turn around when he says this and I know he knows my Da's trying to tell me something. He doesn't turn around and he says, 'I'd rather not have to bring him over to the barracks.'

All the while he's looking at me. Right at me.

Da leaves and as he's passing by me he squeezes my arm just above the elbow. He squeezes and lets go but afterwards I can still feel the impression of each of his fingers, the individual imprint of his thumb. My mouth's going dry and through my mind reflections of everything I've done to warrant a visit from the guards are pinwheeling again. Everything that we, that me and Seán, could have done. They are splinters of broken mirror.

The guard goes, 'Have a seat.'

He goes, 'This shouldn't take too long. Just a few questions that you can help us out with.'

He's not from around here and he has the stretched flatness of the midlands in his voice. I'm sitting down opposite him and my head feels full of rattle and jangle. You know the razor swirls of stuff that corkscrew up when you drill into metal? My head feels full of them. My skull is full of swarf. My thoughts are shrapnel. I'm sitting down opposite him and I'm going, 'What's the problem?'

I'm going, 'Am I in trouble?'

The guard looks at me for a moment and then he's finishing his coffee and then he's taking out a notepad and a pen. He's looking at me and now he's saying, 'No, no I'm sure you're not. If you could just give us some information it'd be appreciated.'

He pronounces his Rs funny. I'm thinking this and I'm sitting at the table and my palms are sweating. I'm sitting at the table and my shirt is starting to stick between my shoulder blades. Seán's violence, Seán's odd behaviour, all of this, is a hot pulse in my chest so that what the guard says next doesn't surprise me. He goes, 'When was the last time you saw your friend Seán Galvin? And when was the last time you saw your neighbour's pigeons?'

It's like this. My neighbours have this pigeon loft built out the back. It's all unpainted timber and rusting nails with a plastic windmill nailed to the roof to take the bare look off it. Its splintered boards are bleached by the weather so that it looks like something you might find on a beach on a tropical island somewhere. A beach hut transported into the wet and cold of Ireland and then flecked with scattered gobs of pigeon shit. The neighbours asked a friend of theirs to mind the birds until they come back from a two-week spell visiting their son in England. They come back and their pigeons have all flown the coop. Literally. According to the guard, Mr and Mrs Redmond haven't seen their pigeons now in days.

This would all be so much so-fucking-what except for Seán. The guard says that they stopped Seán yesterday carrying a pigeon and a string of caps. The ring around the pigeon's leg had been removed so there's no telling for sure who the bird belonged to. But the guard says they're pretty sure they know. What Seán was planning to do with a pigeon and a roll of caps he won't say and the guard can't even imagine.

I tell him, 'I can.'

I tell him that I haven't seen Seán for three days. Not since school on Monday. I tell him I thought he was sick or something. I tell him that at this time of year a lot of people tend to keep their heads down with study and all. I tell him I texted him earlier but I didn't get any reply. I'm telling him all this but what I'm thinking is, I hope the guards don't know about Seán's other stuff.

The guard writes something down and then he goes, 'That's why your neighbours are concerned. Everyone knows that Seán's a little odd and some of those birds were racing pigeons. Quite valuable.'

He says this, *valable*.

I'm shaking my head and I go, 'I honestly don't know, Guard.'

The guard writes something down. And then he goes, 'I take it you two are close. Good mates.'

He says this not as a question and when I nod he writes something down. The way he keeps doing this is starting to make me nervous.

He raises one of his big heavy shovel paws to rub his jaw. The noise it makes is like sellotape. When his hand comes back down he asks did I ever notice anything unusual or threatening in Seán's behaviour.

I tell him no and his writing hand and pen are doing their thing again. I'm not stupid and I'm getting the feeling that the questions are getting more to the point. I'm trying not to panic and I'm trying not to let the fear show in my voice but I don't think I can. Especially when the guard starts talking again.

The guard says that they've already gone through Seán's house and they were wondering why a sixteen-year-old boy would keep so many boxes of old toys in his room. The guard says it's almost like someone was using it as storage space. The guard says that they were wondering why a sixteen-year-old boy would have so many knives.

When he says this it's like the whole kitchen goes dark and pulls away. It's like the walls are exploding away from me and the floor's plummeting and there's only myself and the guard in the middle of this spinning sphere of nothing. My brain refuses to work and I'm finding it hard to breathe.

The guard is looking at me and looking at me and his pen

stabs the notepad and he goes, 'Seán took those pigeons didn't he? At least some of them?'

When old people lose their teeth it's like their mouth is suddenly two sizes too big for their faces. That thing they do when they close their mouth and work their gums against each other, that boneless flexing of the lips is what my mouth is doing now.

From where this comes I don't know, but now I want my Mammy and Daddy.

The guard is taking this all in and he's writing something in his notepad, writing in aggressive, hard strokes. His pen is a heron's beak and it's jabbing and slashing and his eyes never leave my face and I'm wondering what exactly the guard is writing. And I'm wondering, what the fuck has happened to those pigeons? I'm wondering all this and now I'm thinking that we, that me and Seán, are fucked.

The guard doesn't wait for my answer and I'm thinking at this stage he's made his mind up about something. Instead his hand and jaw do their sellotape impression again and he goes, 'We've been asking people living around the Galvins' some questions as well. Asking them about Seán and what they think he's capable of.'

He sits there waiting for a response from me but the only thing I can think of is how Seán's going to hate me for even talking to this guard. He'll never want to speak to me again. To the guard I must look like the way the rabbits look in *Watership Down* when they're frightened. Frozen. Petrified. *Tharn.*

The guard nods to himself and the sharp rasp of his pen is

loud in the no-noise of our kitchen. He's nodding to himself and now he's saying, 'Do you know that we're keeping an eye on your friend, Seán? Do you know that you're the only person he's ever seen hanging around with? You're not afraid that he'll do something that might get the two of you in trouble?'

My stomach is knotting and I'm feeling physically sick and I'm going, 'No. He's my friend.' That last word sticks a bit because I'm not sure if this guard with his sneering expression and his rasping pen could even imagine Seán as a friend in any sense of the word he'd recognise.

The guard goes, 'I see.' And then he's going, 'I had a friend when I was about your age. A Golden Retriever called Ben. Had him for years, since he was a pup.'

I'm looking at the guard and I can see where this is going. I can feel a ball of cold clench in my stomach.

The guard is going, 'Took care of that dog like he was my own brother. I used to mind him when he was sick and take him with me down the fields and all sorts. Shocking nice dog, so he was.'

I'm nodding mechanically, not wanting to think about what he's saying.

The guard just keeps going. He says, 'Lovely animal. Used to follow me everywhere.'

And then the guard lifts the mug to his face and sucks down the last of his coffee and spits out words like he's coughing up phlegm. He goes, 'When he bit the neighbour's youngest, sure we had no option but to put him down.'

His right hand makes a gun with his fingers curled in and his thumb cocked back. His barrel index finger points at me and he says, 'Shot him myself.'

This guard, this big midland farmer's son with his huge hands and thick accent, he goes, 'The next time you see him, tell your friend Seán to mind himself. Tell him that if he were a dog he'd be put down by now.'

And just like that he's getting up and just like that he's putting on his hat and just like that he's leaving by the back door. On the way out he says, 'Thank your Da for the coffee.' On the way out he says, 'We'll be in touch.'

There's a promise in those words. There's a weight of something almost threatening in his voice. It's like when you're little and you know there's something looking at you from the swamp of dark underneath the wardrobe. You can't see it but you know it's there. You can't see it but it can see you.

My Da must hear the back door closing because five seconds after the guard leaves he's back in the kitchen. One side of his hair is messed and one side of his face is rubbed red. I just know that if you get close enough to him you'd see the little dimples made by the woodchip where he's had his ear pressed to the wall. He is a frenzy of every emotion and he's going, 'What was that about? Are you in trouble? Thank God he's gone. Your Ma would be spinning in her grave if she thought you were in trouble. I hope nobody saw him come in.'

I'm not listening to him and I'm not answering him. All I know is that we, that me and Seán, that my life, is all changed. Something's going to have to be done about Seán before he drags us both into the shit. And ignoring my Da, I'm standing up and ignoring him I'm going upstairs and ignoring him I'm sitting on my bed watching the stars get brighter and brighter and I'm listening to Seán's number ring and ring and ring out. Over and over I listen to this pre-programmed voice telling me that I have reached the message minder of 087 blah blah blah. The next time Seán looks at his phone he will have twenty-three missed calls.

This same guard is watching me and Seán and my Da come to a stop in front of Dr Thorpe's porch. In spite of the soft mat of lard that covers his skull, his face looks like it's been quarried out of something like flint and he's not smiling. He's not smiling but there's this glimmer in his eyes like he's giggling away to himself on the inside. I'm looking at him and I bet that inside his skull there's nothing but a gale of laughter.

He goes, 'The gruesome twosome.'

And then he turns and then he and Dr Thorpe are chuckling together like they're old college buddies or something. The only things missing are the cigars and brandy.

And just like that I know no one's going to believe us.

Dr Thorpe is standing there dressed in this red dressing gown. His hair's still as pristine as ever but he's obviously just had a shower or hosed himself down or something because his skin is still wet and it's soaking through the material of the gown. The material is probably supposed to be an arterial scarlet sort of colour but now it's drenched into a matt, scabrous madder.

Da pushes between the guard and Dr Thorpe and he shakes hands with the two of them. He's gurning like he's been lobotomised and the only thing he isn't doing is tugging his forelock or fucking genuflecting.

He's going, 'Jaysus, I'm sorry, Guard. I'm sorry Doctor.'

He knifes a look over his shoulder at me and Seán. We're standing there like shop mannequins with our skin cold and slick as plastic. I can hear the drone of Seán's moaning. The faraway beehive sound of his unease. Right now, right at this minute, I hate my Da.

He's going, 'Young fellahs. Always messing. Sure, we may lock them up or something, hagh.'

He grins first at the guard then at Dr Thorpe and then back at the guard again.

They both smile back at him but their smiles have a different quality to the one that's creasing my Da's face. I've seen those smiles before when a child does something stupid or awkward, their motor skills only developed enough to drop things or smear themselves with jam. Their parents look down and they smile. It's all so cute. This is what Dr Thorpe and the guard look like. Like parents indulging a squaling child.

I've had enough of this and I go, 'Guard, I was the one who rang the barracks. I believe I've witnessed a murder.'

The three adults, the doctor, the guard and my Da, all three, exchange this half-amused, half-exasperated look. Dr Thorpe makes this disgusting little sound that's halfway between a snort and a laugh and looking at him I can see his fist come cracking down over his right shoulder like the fall of a sledge.

The guard turns to me and Seán and he goes, 'That's quite a claim to be making. Who witnessed this "murder" exactly?'

Before I can say anything Dr Thorpe goes, 'Can we have this conversation inside the house, please, Ted? It's bad enough having your car parked in my drive without words like that being bandied about the place.'

The guard grins at me and Seán without any kind of humour. Great White Sharks are way heavier than you think and when you see them on wildlife programmes you can see how massive their heads are. They've got these big, fat, wide heads, all muscle and snaggle-teeth. The guard's grinning head reminds me of this.

He looks at my Da and goes, 'I have no objection to that. Do you?'

Da's shaking his head and he's saying, 'God, no. Work away.'

Seán's groaning goes up a notch and he starts spilling words from his worm-red lips. He's saying, 'I don't want to. I don't want to.'

Over and over again he says this until the guard goes, 'We could get your Da down here too, Seán? Would you like that? Do you think he'd be happy?'

Seán's voice stops working like all the air has been sucked out of his lungs. His lips wriggle for a second and then they press together and go pale. He shakes his head, once, deliberately.

Dr Thorpe steps aside and all the light and all the heat of his big house comes pouring down the throat of his hallway and empties out into dank of the night. Me and Seán go in past him with our heads bowed. Like slaves bent under iron chains, beaten and spiritless, the two of us step into the hall. We, me and Seán, are careful not to touch Dr Thorpe as we go by him. You can smell the scent of freshly-scrubbed skin coming off him, that and the permanent chemical reek of hairspray.

He smiles down at us and he says, 'Welcome to my humble abode.'

Behind us the guard comes in and then my Da comes in and then Dr Thorpe is shutting the front door.

Dr Thorpe's hallway extends off in front of us and everything is all mellow wood and beeswax and cream paint. Everything is from page fourteen of the Dulux colour scheme brochure. Everything is *Barley Mist* and *Summer Oat* and *Buttermilk Sheen*. Everything is off-white. It is the colour of baby vomit.

My Da is looking around and he's going, 'Very nice, Doctor. Very tasteful.'

Down the hall, where it opens up into the kitchen I can see the spot where I saw Dr Thorpe and that woman. Him lying on top of her. Her face bleeding. It all comes back and it's like I'm going to throw up.

The dead meat smack of it.

Now there's no sign of what happened. No blood. No sweat streaks on the floorboards. Nothing to suggest anything happened. It's as though I imagined the whole thing.

Seán's looking at me and his face is pale and lax.

Dr Thorpe shows us all into a side room. The room is a kind of study with shelves all around the walls and a desk and six or seven chairs set about the place. The shelves are crammed with books and on the desk there's one of those brass lamps with the green glass hoods. The lamp is on and the glass glows the colour of cat eyes. There are golf trophies on nearly every flat surface and there's a special plaque sitting on the desk next to the lamp. In the light the engraved lettering is all swilled with sepia. It reads *Strawberry Fair Golf Classic Winner 2009 2010 2011*. In the middle of the floor sits my gear bag, covered in dried muck and grass stains with my name inked in black on the red panelling.

I'm looking at the bag and then Dr Thorpe goes, 'Gentlemen, if you could all take a seat we can clear this matter right up.'

Seán looks at me and I go, 'I'd prefer to stand.'

Seán's nodding and he folds his arms the way mine are folded.

Da sighs then and he says, 'Don't be stupid. Would you sit down for fuck's sake.'

Then he seems to remember where he is and he goes, 'Pardon my French.'

The guard slaps him on the shoulder like they're suddenly best friends and he goes, 'Don't worry about it. This is very stressful for everyone.'

Then everyone else, except me and Seán, sits down.

Still standing, I go, 'Should we not be doing this down at the barracks or something?'

Then everyone else, except me and Seán, shake their heads like I've started speaking in tongues.

The guard, with a sort of mockery gusting through his voice, goes, 'Who exactly saw what here, lads?'

Seán's not stupid and he knows we're getting the piss taken out of us and I can feel him tensing up. He's afraid and he's angry and I can feel the potential in him.

Before Seán can say, or worse, do, anything, I'm saying, 'I saw it. I saw him over there hitting and choking a girl.'

The doctor looks uncomfortable at this and under his breath I hear the word *preposterous* slink out from between his lips. He reaches up and adjusts the fall of his bathrobe and he crosses his bare, white ankles. He is wearing slippers. In his chair with his wet red robe he looks like a massive haematoma or a huge tick, swollen and bloated with blood.

The guard is rubbing his forehead and he's going, 'How did you manage to see this alleged incident?'

Talking quickly now, I'm going, 'We came up along the driveway and we heard a noise. I looked in the letterbox—'

My Da explodes at this and his face is all wrinkled and red like a fresh scar. He says, 'You did what? You were spying through a letterbox like some sort of pervert? Wait till I get you home.'

I'm shocked and I'm blinking at my Da and Seán brings his hands up to his face. I can't believe my Da. I can't believe he's leaving me twisting in the wind like this.

Before I can say anything, before I can defend myself, Dr Thorpe goes, 'Ted, I'm going to say this right now that I'm not going to press charges against these lads. I don't think they meant any harm. I just want to know what they were doing on my doorstep.'

I'm looking from my Da to Dr Thorpe to the guard and then back. First one, then the other, then the other. It's like my muscles are on a loop. I'm like some broken android, almost human but not quite.

I'm wondering, how the hell did this happen? How did it end up that me and Seán are the bad guys?

He's not going to press charges against *us*?

The guard is looking at me and Seán now and he goes, 'Why were you here, lads? The doctor says his gates were locked. What would make you climb over the wall? That's trespass. You do realise that?'

He looks at Seán, Seán with his face buried in the crooked fingers of both hands, and his eyes narrow and he goes, 'What have you been up to Mr Galvin?'

Seán begins to groan and the whole room, padded and walled with books and arch intellectualism, now makes echo to his inarticulate pain.

The guard is grinning again and his lips are hooked at the corners like a pike's and he goes, 'Are you going to tell me, Seán? If you tell me maybe we can help you.'

And Seán's voice, all sticky and soft like marl, Seán's voice comes between his fingers and he goes, 'I did a bad thing. A really really bad thing.'

And just like that Dr Thorpe sits back in his chair and the

guard smiles across at him. My Da is looking in disgust at Seán and in his head I know every atom of dislike he has towards him is bouncing off every other atom and making a supernova of bad feeling.

All of a sudden it's like Dr Thorpe has won and we, me and Seán, have lost.

I'm really pissed off now and I snap at Dr Thorpe, 'I know what I saw.'

And like someone out of *Scooby Doo*, I go, 'You won't get away with this.'

My Da is sitting forward in his chair and I can see he's pissed off too but it's the guard who says something. He says, 'Let's all calm down now for a minute. It's obvious the boys are upset about whatever Seán here's gotten up to.'

I'm turning from person to person and Seán's no help buried behind the ramparts of his hands and I'm going, 'You don't understand. What I saw has nothing to do with Seán. I'm not making this up. I wouldn't do that.'

Da goes, 'Don't, son.'

He says this at the exact same time as the guard goes, 'Really? Mr Trustworthy all of a sudden, yeah?'

He leans forward in his chair and I can see Dr Thorpe start to smile as the guard goes, 'Tell us what happened last summer.'

Remember when I said that I was grand and that Seán's internal wiring was badly fused? Well that's still true, definitely true, but I did get in a bit of trouble last summer. Not out of badness or any-thing. It was more a practical joke that got out of hand.

I worked in an office for the summer. An insurance place right on the Market Square. My Da knows the broker. Two other lads worked there. Both were doing honours degrees in business and something money spinning. They photocopied. They made coffee. They were patronised. They could run the place. They didn't.

I do pretty well in Business in school. I hate doing hard sums but marketing and stuff like that I'm really good at. I don't know what I'm going to do when I leave school. Probably something Englishy. After that I can take my degree and go to a bank for a job. With my English degree I can stand at a photocopier while the green lightsabre blade traverses beneath its glass and pro-duces ever more faded copies of the original. Everything in an office is a copy of a copy of a copy. Nothing is ever original. If you're really lucky you can fiddle with the finishing buttons on the photocopier until you figure out how to actually staple the copies as they're vomiting out. This is a big deal. It can save you hours of pointless stapling and leave you free to produce ever more copies of Declaration A.

See also Declaration B.

See also Direct Debit Mandates.

I am a tongueless bell.

I am a waste of potential.

I have a certain smug satisfaction in knowing that I found the photocopier's stapler before the Commerce students did. I am one rung higher up the corporate ladder than they are. One rung higher up and I'm still drowning in shit.

This happy little vista does naught for the nascent professionalism which a young buck like myself should nurture. Shortly before the end of the summer I'm let go. Nothing is said to Da except the work was drying up. Nothing was said but I'm pretty sure he knows.

The insurance place that I was let go from has a big plate glass window that looks out onto the Market Square. During the summer people move in a flux past it without ever looking in. An insurance place does not tend to attract window shoppers. I stand at the back of the office and I look out over the heads of six people sitting in cubicles and I watch other people walk in sunshine, oblivious to anyone in here. Outside the office, the people's faces are angry, worried, smiling, blank. Human. Each couple that passes is a soap opera. Each individual a soliloquy.

There's the young couple barely in their thirties. He's carrying the shopping that has obviously been shopped for by her. His sky-blue T-shirt has darkened in a cobalt fan under the arms and he's standing behind her as she stops to take something out of her purse. She can't seem to stop talking and the look of hatred on his face is scary. Then she's turning and then she's kissing him on the cheek. His face is now a mask of bovine contentedness. But I remember the way he looked when her back was turned. He is an animal in a cage.

Then there's the young fella who just came out of the hairdresser's. He can't be any more than ten or so and his arm makes a hard bony triangle over his head because he's trying to get at something itchy down the back of his tracksuit top. His head is shaven down to almost stubble and his skin shows through pale and domed over his skull. He is small and thin and now his head looks too big for his body. With his angry little face and bundle of sticks body he looks like a cross between a skinhead and an Auschwitz victim. A conflation of opposites. His whole being is a contradiction in terms. With a complete lack of self-consciousness he stands in front of the plate glass window and looks at his reflection. His hand comes out of the back of his top and rubs delicately over the bristles of his head. He doesn't see anyone in here and no one in here sees him. Except me.

The office works like this. A bank tells someone they need insurance to get a mortgage. This aforementioned someone comes to the insurance office and fills out a proposal form for Life and Serious Illness cover or Mortgage Protection or both, ensuring it's signed and dated on the Xs.

See also Declaration A.

See also Declaration B.

See also Direct Debit Mandate.

Now, strictly speaking, just to get a quote from an insurance company not everything has to be filled in. You can leave out certain details. Not details like whether you're on the verge of croaking from motor neuron disease or details like the fact that the tumour pulsing in your brain has just been diagnosed as inoperable. Not stuff like that. But to just get a quote you can leave out other details.

Usually underneath the personal details there's a little empty field marked *Occupation*. This is there so that if someone like a scaffolder wants insurance the insurance company can screw them over because they work at a height. If the poor fuck falls three storeys off his scaffolding there's a fair chance he'll either be dead as dead can be or not really in any condition to continue working. In the industry this is called *risk*. Outside the industry this is still called *risk*. The insurance cover is there so that if he can't meet the mortgage repayments through injury or falling from a height and impaling himself on rebar the bank still gets paid.

Financial Institutions 1 : Everyone Else 0.

Myself and the business undergrads who work in the office collect up the proposals that are filled in. We photocopy them for the files. Then we either post them or fax them to the insurance company. This is what we do. All day every day. Some days you can actually feel your brain turning to sludge. I'm starting to find it difficult to make abstract connections anymore. My eyes are sore from the photocopier's glare. Then I do something just to prove I can still change the routine, to prove I can still invent things. I do something that gets me fired.

Once more with feeling. This isn't done out of badness and this isn't anything like the stuff that Seán does.

There's a stack of proposals left on the edge of a table to be photocopied and sent off. I know this because there's a pink post-it stuck to the top one with the words PHOTOCOPY & SEND OFF written on it. Every day there's another post-it curling up from the top of another pile of proposals and every day it says the same thing. You'd think we wouldn't need instructions by now. The proposals are always a pleasing peach colour and the parts you fill in are all white squares for the BLOCK CAPITALS. Most people ignore the block capitals thing and simply scrawl the information across the boxes. Each proposal is a smudged mess of blue or black ink. The pink post-it though is always clearly printed in BLOCK CAPITALS.

Most days as I'm working through the stack I check some of the proposals. Mainly I do this because otherwise I'll go insane. I just run my eye over the names, the addresses, the dates of birth. Sometimes if a date of birth or something important is missing we get flak from head office. There's a middle-aged, nervous person who works here, named Sarah. If head office gets Sarah on a bad day she starts to cry and has to have a fag and a cup of tea before she can face work again. I could say I check the proposals in order to postpone Sarah's imminent nervous breakdown but I'd be lying. I couldn't give a flying fuck about either Sarah or head office. Nobody knows this though and when I spot something wrong I get a pat on the head and am cooed over. I am a novelty act. I am a performing seal.

The *Occupation* part of the proposal form always draws my attention. Maybe I'm just nosey but a lot of people who fill in these forms are local so I probably know them. Mostly, there's the usual mix of farmers, general operatives and the oddly repellent sounding *house duties*. Every so often though you get a novelist or artist and I'm thinking, who are these people? Where do they live? Why haven't I heard of them? Provincial towns don't tend to produce bohemian types. The atmosphere of spent ambition, of time's slow coalescence, means that aspirations beyond farmer or general operative are stillborn. Strangled at birth. People give up. No one is ever a poet.

See also Sculptor.

See also Actor.

See also Playwright.

I decide to give people an occupation.

I go through the stack of proposals, pen in hand, waiting until I see a blank *Occupation* section. I look around and as usual no one is looking at me. Sarah is putting down the phone and is starting to cry. She is having a bad day. Everyone else is either transfixed by their computer screens or is starting to gravitate towards the wreck that is Sarah's sobbing body.

I come to a proposal with a blank *Occupation* section. Now I'm reading the name and address and date of birth and now I'm writing. The proposal belongs to one Mr Alexander O'Sullivan who lives in Kiltealy. He is forty-eight years of age and now he works as a drug dealer. I don't intend to make him a drug dealer. At first I'm going to make him a musician but then I'm thinking, why should I? Maybe it's jealousy but I'm not going to give this place another artist in hiding. I want to bring everyone down to zero. I'm looking out the window at the smiling, blank, defeated faces, the vacant lot of human existence. And I decide to make people what I see. Again, not out of badness, I decide to make people the rotten core at the heart of everything. I think it'd be funny. I think that I'm somehow proving my intellectual superiority. So I make them drug dealers. So I make them pimps. So I make them human detritus.

See also Rent Boys.

See also People Traffickers.

See also Thieves.

Each time I come across a doctor, a surgeon, an artist I strike a line through their occupation and put in something else. Then I photocopy them and then I send them off. Behind me Sarah is sobbing and someone's going, 'It's okay, it's alright. It's not your fault.'

How I get sacked from the insurance place is like this. Every day I go through the stack of proposals and every day I give people new occupations. Every day I look out on the Market Square and watch the random melodrama of human life and every day I drag more and more people into the gutter.

During the summer, purple and gold bunting goes up and people with purple and gold jerseys come in and go out. Women walk by with the inevitable *Wexford Creamery* printed across their tits. Summer brings this year after year. A fat farmer wearing a jersey so small it looks like it's sprayed on has just handed in a proposal and, quick as a flash, I tippex out Dairy Farmer from the occupation field and put in Pornographer. I can't help myself.

Again, this is not done out of badness.

Sarah spends half the summer crying and smoking and drinking tea. Her tears must taste like tobacco and tannin. Her teeth are turning yellow.

Outside people move in clumps or alone. Everyone moves in sunshine. Everyone is smiling. In here the computers spew out radiation and everyone is smiling except me and the business undergrads. We are photocopying and sending off. There are targets to be met.

Trouble starts because of Dr Thorpe.

The procedure goes like this.

When a person applies for Life and Serious Illness cover or Mortgage Protection the proposal is sent off to head office for assessment and processing. Depending on the answers that the client gives to the questions on the nice peach and white forms it goes to underwriting. Depending on the answers that the client gives to the questions on the nice peach and white forms a medical report is requested. This is to ensure that the client isn't going to die of throat cancer or renal failure any time soon.

See also Leukaemia.

See also Muscular Dystrophy.

See also Heart Disease.

One of the items that determine this is what the client's occupation is listed as.

I don't know who Elaine Doyle is. I don't care who Elaine Doyle is. But it is because of Elaine Doyle that I get sacked.

Elaine Doyle is a lab technician. For all her working life she has been a lab technician and now according to the records of a certain life assurance company she is a high-class prostitute. This is quite a career move for a woman in her thirties.

I can't remember doing this to her. Then again I can never

remember individual names. All these proposals, all these lives, are one homogenous slick of sewage. Outside walking in the sunshine are factory workers, butchers, shop assistants and in the silicone depths of our database they are human waste. They are holes in the day. They are shadows in the sunlight. I'm standing at the desk watching them through the big front window. I've a black pen in my right hand and I'm about to have a quick rifle through today's proposals. There's a hugely fat couple laughing with each other in the middle of the road and I'm wondering what they work at. The woman has *Wexford Creamery* stretched across her chest.

It is at this moment that the shit hits the fan.

The broker, the person who owns this bustling establishment, steps out onto the office floor. Then he's turning to me and he's going, 'Would you mind having a word with me in private, please?' It's the *in private* bit that gets me. I've never, ever, seen him pass up the opportunity to humiliate someone in public.

I follow him into his office and I close the door behind me. I'm wondering what he wants and now I'm thinking how this can't be good. There's a letter lying on his desk and upside down I'm reading it and upside-down I can see the signature. It says Dr S. Thorpe. I'm reading this and for some reason I'm trying to stop myself laughing. And now I'm wondering what the main part of the letter says.

I'm standing here with the broker looking at me with this prim expression pursing his mouth so that it looks almost sutured shut. He's looking at me and his left hand is pulsing on the desk beside the letter. It is spotted and crawled over with thick veins. It is a grotesque spider, hairless and scrawny and straining with tension. I'm standing here and behind the broker venetian blinds segment the day and I'm trying to stop myself laughing.

The three paragraphs of Dr S. Thorpe's letter probably go something along the lines of: Mrs Doyle has been a patient of mine for blah blah I have never known her to be employed as anything other than blah blah Mrs Doyle and, indeed, I, as her doctor am shocked blah blah grossly embarrassing blah blah HIV Test blah blah Internal Examination blah blah Legal Action blah blah. Blah.

I can't read this. Upside-down it is Cyrillic but looking at the broker and the urgent blind spider of his left hand I know this is what it says. Looking at the broker and his puckered sphincter of a mouth I know this is the end of my life in the fast-paced world of insurance brokerage. I can't say I'm exactly despondent over this and now I can feel the start of a smile leak out from the edges of my lips. It is a guilty stain.

Now the broker's face is going blood clot purple and something's making a fault line in the middle of his forehead. He's looking like he's about to explode and he's looking like he's about to kill me and then his face is going pale again. The pink and knuckled spider on the desk is uncurling itself and I'm starting to grin.

Then he's picking up the letter and then he's putting it back down and then he's saying stuff. He's saying, 'I'm not even going to ask you if you did this. That shit-eating expression of yours says everything.'

And now I'm realising that he hates me. Right here right now he hates me more than anything. And now I'm wondering how long it will take before he hits me. I'm suddenly worried. Offices are full of potential lethal weapons; scissors, paperweights, letter openers. That kind of thing. It's only the weirdly constipated expression on his face that keeps me grinning.

He's going, 'Yeah I fucking knew it was you. As soon as I opened this fucking letter, I knew it had to be a little fucking smart arse like you.'

I'm just standing there. I get the feeling that this rant is going better than he thought. He's leaning forward in his chair now and his head is a spitting white-hot ball bearing and he's saying, 'The others wouldn't fuck up a great chance like this. Fucking summer workers, you're all the same. Jesus Christ, I do a favour for your Da and you wouldn't even make a fucking go of it.' Now I'm wondering, a fucking go of what? Of stapling?

See also Photocopying.

See also Making Coffee.

See also Counting Petty Cash.

He's sitting in his chair and if this were a cartoon little jets of steam would be whistling out of his ears. He's sitting in his chair and if this were a TV programme I'd try to explain why I did this to Elaine Doyle amongst others. He's sitting in his chair with his back to the day and on his desk there's the letter, two pens, a calendar, a Waterford Crystal paperweight and his computer. He's sitting at his desk and he's going, 'Do you have anything to say for yourself?'

I'm looking at him and now I'm articulating six words, 'I'm surprised this is the first.'

Then I'm ducking and the paperweight misses my head by inches.

This all seemed quite jolly last year. Now with my Da staring at the floor and the guard grinning nastily at me it doesn't seem so funny. Dr Thorpe is sitting in his chair with a smile creeping across his face like something seeping out from under an abattoir door. The light in here is dim and isn't like the halogen glare of the rest of the house. All it seems to be doing is emphasising the gloom gathered in the corners and the heavy walls of books all around. I'm suddenly feeling claustrophobic and my lips are crinkling up like dead leaves and going all dry.

Into the silence, into the awkward gap opened up by the guard's question, my Da goes, 'Alright, Guard. That's enough. We get your point.'

I go to say something back but now my Da is looking at me and I can see something hot and flaring in his eyes. He's saying, 'And can you not be such a little prick all the time? Now you're in this as well as Seán and nobody can believe the Lord's prayer out of either of you. So just spit it out. What were the two of you doing here spying through a fucking letterbox?'

This time he doesn't apologise for his language and beside him

Dr Thorpe has this expression on his face like a Pope handing out blessings. Dr Thorpe had that same fucking expression all the time when he came to see Mam. The night she died it was there like the skin over a blister. I remember that and now me and Seán just stand here in front of him like we're up in front of a judge. Me and Seán just stand there and the unfairness of it all nearly has me in tears. The memory of my Mam weighs down on me. Sixteen years of age and it's like I'm about to break down crying.

The guard nods at me and Seán and he says, 'We'll get to the bottom of things quicker if you just tell us the whole story. It'll go easier on you.'

And I'm thinking, you're all bastards. Every adult in this fucking town is a dick. *It'll go easier on you*, my arse.

And all the time Dr Thorpe just sits there looking at the two of us like a curious spectator. The fact of his violence, the hidden awfulness of what he is, is sitting in my stomach like an ulcer.

The dead meat smack of it.

I know he's going to do it before he does it. Beside me Seán cracks and beside me he goes, 'I'm really sorry. Really really sorry.'

In spite of my indignation. In spite of my anger at how powerless we are. In spite of the fact that nobody belives us. In spite of all this, Seán can't keep it in anymore. I listen as he talks and with every word he says I can feel any hope we have of seeing Dr Thorpe taken away in handcuffs disappear. Every word he says knocks the steel out of me bit by bit and I can feel myself sagging. Physically sagging. Worse than this I can feel my mind playing tricks on me. I'm standing there listening to Seán talk about what he did to those dogs and I'm wondering, did I actually see anything at all? Did I see Dr Thorpe, smiling, talk-show Dr Thorpe, actually strangle someone? Am I going nuts?

All the adults are listening to Seán and he's almost sobbing now. He's sobbing with relief and his words are roped all together with mucus and he's snuffling because the shame and disgust he's carrying around with him is being purged. It's like Dr Thorpe's study is a confessional and Seán wants nothing but to be absolved.

All the adults are listening to Seán and expressions are sleeting one after another across their faces. My Da is sitting there and his face seems to be all concern and reassurance but he can't hide the curl of his lip and the weird wrinkle of his nose. He can't hide how appalled he is by Seán. He doesn't want them to but his eyes keep flicking to the dark stains on Seán's jacket and I know he's remembering the smell he got in our hallway. The guard is sitting forward in his chair with his forearms braced on his thighs and his pudding fingers bundled together like he's praying. He's nodding in fake plastic understanding and his head is doing that horrible insincere bobbing thing that adults do when they're patronising someone. But in his face and in the set of his shoulders I can see that he's delighted at this. Every single suspicion he's had about Seán Galvin has been confirmed and laid out in front of him. Each one spelled out in an augury of spilled entrails. And Dr Thorpe just sits in his bloody robe. Sits and radiates sympathy. Lord of his domain.

When Seán finishes, Dr Thorpe goes, 'We'll need to put you on some rather stronger medication, Seán. I'm sorry the other prescription didn't work as well as I'd hoped.'

And the guard goes, 'I'm sorry for disturbing you, Dr Thorpe. This was a waste of everyone's time.'

Dr Thorpe looks at him and smiles and says, 'No problem, Ted. Sure, aren't we all here to serve. If Seán gets the help he needs out of this, well then at least some good has been done.'

Da doesn't say anything. He's just looking at Seán like he's seen him for the first time.

I can't say anything. I've never felt so beaten. I've never felt so worthless. How this has happened I don't know but all my fucking arrogance has been misplaced. Nobody takes me seriously. Not just Seán, but *us*. I'm suddenly as big a fuck-up as he is. I'm a sixteen-year-old child getting laughed at by people who know more than me. The limits of what I can do are now clearly defined and set out for me and what they amount to is shag all.

And all the while Dr Thorpe is smiling his smile and then he winks at me. Slowly and carefully. A *we know something that they don't know* sort of wink.

And now I'm thinking, I'm going to get you, you smug arsehole. You're going to regret this.

When Dr Thorpe shuts the front door he straightaway turns off the porch light. Me and Seán and my Da and the guard are all suddenly drenched in dark. Skin looks blue without light and the guard's big moon face turns to me, turns to Seán, turns to my Da.

The guard shakes his head and then says to my Da, 'Can we have a little chat?'

The two of them go over to the squad car and me and Seán are left standing on the porch. I have my stupid gear bag slung on my back again and Seán is still sniffling and I'm going, 'Would you cut that out.'

Seán shakes his head like a dog drying itself and he goes, 'I had to tell them. My head was all full of stuff. I couldn't listen to them talk anymore.'

I'm watching the guard and my Da mutter to each other. The guard has his big blue-sleeved arm around my Da's scrawny shoulders. I don't look at Seán but I'm saying, 'I know. You're in a bad way. I know you feel bad about the dead dogs. I don't blame you for anything.'

Seán nods slowly and then he says, 'Dr Thorpe thinks he got away with it.'

And just like that I know why I'm friends with Seán. He never doubts me. He doesn't say, *You never saw anything.* He doesn't say, *Dr Thorpe wouldn't do something like that.* He doesn't say, *Nobody can believe the Lord's prayer out of you.* He trusts me.

And then Seán goes, 'I don't want to take any more tablets he gives me but I don't want to do any more bad things.'

I'm looking at him now and I go, 'I don't know what we're going to do, Seán.'

The guard and my Da are walking back towards us now and before they get to us Seán says, 'Nobody believes us.'

And I go, 'No. They don't.'

Then my Da is standing in front of us and he's saying, 'Garda Devlin said he'll give us a lift home. We'll drop you out first, Seán.'

Seán's house is out the Still Road beyond Cherry Orchard. We have to pass our old house on the way to it. My Da is sitting in the passenger seat of Guard Devlin's squad car and between him and the guard the shiny plastic block of the radio bleeps and lights up. Every so often a squawk of static erupts from it and you can hear voices all tinny and distorted saying stuff. The guard has it turned down though so you can't get any sense of what obscure dramas are going on around town as we rumble out the Milehouse Road and swing left at the Aldi roundabout. The static of the radio is the only sound in the car. Otherwise we're travelling along in a little box of inarticulate tension.

When we pass our old house I twist like something caught on a hook so that I can catch a glimpse of our old garden. The new owners have cut back the ditches and my Mam's flower beds have all been dug up and grassed over. We drive past but my head keeps swivelling. My gaze is tethered to our old house. Big, heavy hawsers of memory and laughter tie me to it. I'm sitting watching my childhood race away through the rear windscreen and I can feel myself go limp. The sight of the house like this has me not just hooked. It has me gaffed and gutted.

Seán's driveway is short and it's concreted over and leads down to an old dormer bungalow with a glass and plastic conservatory thrusting out from one gable wall. It's dark now but in the day you can see the green mould and the drifts of dead flies that cram the angles of the conservatory windows. Seán's Da hasn't really been paying attention to the little things for the last while.

When the front door opens Seán's Da is standing there and against the light from the hall you can't see his face but you can make out the stoop of his shoulders. You can make out the lack of surprise at the sight of a squad car in his yard. You can make out the resignation that weeps from him.

Seán gets out of the squad car and walks past him into the house and just like that Seán's front door is hammering closed. His Da doesn't acknowledge us. He doesn't say anything to anyone, just slams the door shut on himself and his fucked-up son.

My Da and Guard Devlin exchange a look but they don't say anything to each other and they definitely don't say anything to me.

The guard swings the car around and its headlights splash across the front of Seán's house, splash across the ditches and bushes along the drive and now they're splashing out across concrete and tarmac. In their light everything is given brittle edges and the shadows behind things are intensified. It looks like the entire world is one huge page from a giant pop-up book. In the headlights the whole place looks two-dimensional and backed by nothing but empty space.

When we get home Da thanks the guard and apologises for my behaviour and then he drags me inside the house. Before I can say anything he goes, 'You're not seeing that Galvin boy until he gets put on his new meds. Do you hear me?'

I blink at him and say nothing. I hate this.

By the time I see Seán again his black eye is starting to fade into the yellow colour of a thunderhead.

Without Seán, I have nothing to do. I spend the next couple of days avoiding my Da. I try not to think about Dr Thorpe's fist crashing into the brittle cartilage and soft blubber of that woman's face. Again and again and again. The dead meat smack of it. I try to not think of the spark that I saw go out in her. I try not to wonder what Dr Thorpe has done with her. My dreams are full of clutching hands and the smell of fake pine. They are full of voices saying, 'Shhhhhhhhhh.'

Two days later I ring the guards again and the voice at the other end of the line goes, 'Is this about that yoke with Dr Thorpe? Listen chap, Garda Devlin has that under control.' And then the line goes dead and I'm left holding the receiver and staring at it while it beeeeeeeeeps at me.

Garda fucking Devlin.

I think about going down the Banks and then I think better of it. Seán isn't in school all week and he doesn't reply to my texts and his Facebook page is shut down. I don't know what's happening to him but I'd say there's doctors involved. I'm really worried and every time I see a squad car I want to run and hide.

Sunday morning I wake up in a sweat and I'm breathing so hard I sound like Ronan Davitt who has asthma so bad he never, ever, does P.E. I'm lying there in bed and I'm wondering, am I having a panic attack? Is this what post-traumatic stress feels like? I'm swinging my legs over the side of the bed and I can hear my Da rattling around in the back yard. And just like that I decide to go watch the men's team playing their football match. This has as much to do with the fact that I can't talk to my Da anymore as it does with the fact that I like football.

When I was younger I used to play with the club I play for because it was only down the road from me. I used to play with this club until we left our house out by the Still. When that happened something changed and I stopped playing for a while. I went back to them last season though because I can't play with any other club. It doesn't feel right.

Now from our shitty little house the pitch is about a thirty minute walk which is a bitch if it's wet and cold but today it's nice so I don't mind. The season is heading into the last maybe eight games or so and when I look at the league tables in the paper I see the men's team is doing pretty well. Nine more points and they should get promoted and I'm smiling at this. I'm happy for a group of people to which I don't really have any connection except that they wear the same colour jersey as me. I'm thinking that no matter where you go you always carry something of where you're from with you. Like someone exposed to MRSA.

The pitch is really two pitches with an all-weather training area for the men's teams alongside. The men's training pitch is surfaced with stuff like aggregate. The only difference between it and the car park is you'd laugh at someone who said you were going to slide and scrape around on the car park for two hours. If you go right up close to the training pitch and look at the gouges torn into it I swear you can see scraps of skin left behind. The elephant wrinkles of elbows and knees. The tender stuff of palms. People rip themselves up on this patch of ground so they don't lose Sunday League matches on the nice patch of grass over there. Maybe it shouldn't, and to a lot of people it doesn't, but to anyone involved this makes perfect sense.

The town on Sunday mornings is hushed like something drugged. Walking through the Square there's a few tattered rags of chip papers lying around and an empty burger carton goes skirling away across the path when the breeze catches it. The inside of the burger carton is splatted with ketchup and curved slivers of onion. The only people stirring at this time are the people going to matches all red-eyed and bleary. The ones who were on the tear last night are swollen-faced and heavy-jowled and they look around themselves with appalled frankness, like for the first time they can see the world exactly as it really is. The only people stirring at this time are the people going to matches and the threadbare line of alcos waiting outside Barrett's Pub at the top of the town. Half-nine on a Sunday morning and there's people queuing for a snakey pint. Just to take the hard edge off the day.

I'm walking past this shambling line of patchwork people and then I'm standing beside the pitch watching the lads kick around before the game starts and then I'm screaming something out over the Market Square. It's funny how things turn out.

The two teams out there are both local and both sets of players know each other. Both sets of players know each other both on and off the pitch. Both sets of players hate each other both on and off the pitch. This is because the other team are scum. This state of affairs does not bode well for the match as a spectacle of Barcelona-style passing and movement. It does however bode well for the match as a spectacle of kicking and off-the-ball incidents.

In much the same way as a car crash attracts the morbidly curious there's a fairly big crowd standing around. I'm next to a lad I used to play with before he went off to college last year and we're talking shite and we're watching the two teams kick fucking lumps out of each other. Then this lad, this lad who's two or three years older than me, turns to me. He turns to me and he goes, 'Jesus would you look at that other shower. The state of them. Wife-beaters and drug-dealers. Fucking dirtbags.'

He's looking at the pitch and his eyes flick to every opposition shirt and he's saying, '"Sure what would you want a job for?" Fucking spastics.'

I don't know what's happened to this lad with his red hair and his freckles. I don't know what's been done to him but he's spitting these words out and the way his eyes are looking from jersey to jersey is a little scary. This lad's nearly an architect and had to work hard to get it. It's like the ignorance branded on some of the faces out there is a personal insult to him.

We stand there watching the rest of the match and we don't say much else. Injuries happen and the crowd becomes a bristling hedge of spittle and vitriol. I'm not thinking about them. I'm not really paying any attention to the game anymore. What my ex-teammate said has settled into my brain. It is something barbed.

I'm looking around and it's like I'm back in the insurance place again. The crowd watching the game has become one big blank to me. The faces, laughing, shouting, cheering, are like scar tissue in my eyes. Smooth, flat, numb.

The lads win 2–1 and I'm looking happy and smiling because this is what I'm supposed to look like. In my head a wound is opening. No matter what I do, I can't get rid of the sound of fist on flesh. It's way more solid than you think. You know when you watch a film and the hero swings and connects with a big round-house punch? You know that sharp crack of a sound that they add in post-production? Well that's complete bullshit because it doesn't sound anything at all the way that Dr Thorpe's fist sound-ed as it jack-knifed down into that woman's face. There's a weight and there's a concussion to it that's sickening.

One of the lads in school has a video on his iPhone of some poor bastard in Chechnya being beheaded. I can watch it as far as where the knife slides into his gullet and this stuff like black ink starts to run out of his mouth. He can't even scream because the psycho doing this is sawing through his voice box. I can only watch so far because I start to feel fucking faint and honest to God I think I'm going to throw up all over the resource area.

This doesn't surprise me but Seán watches it all the way through.

This is how I feel all the time now. I feel like the stomach has fallen out of the world and there's a big hole that I keep filling with fear and disgust until it overflows and starts drowning everything else. I'm trying to force the hollowness that's yawning all around me to pucker closed for a bit. Imagine a bullet wound or an incision for a surgical drain. Imagine the way that looks when it heals. Corrugated around the edges, plugged with scar tissue but a weak point all the same. That's what my life is now. I'm standing watching the lads huff and slop off the field and I'm trying to draw everything tight about the hole in my life. I'm trying to seal it but it's still there.

Seán hasn't rang or texted all week and when I come home from the match he still hasn't rang or texted. I don't like this and I'm getting the feeling that my life is starting to flap loose like the edge of a burst blister. I get home and walk into the kitchen and my aunt is there and she's saying to Da, 'We have to talk about him.' Then she stops and then she looks at me and then she pretends to do something with the cooker. Fuck her. Da's clearing his throat and now he's going to say something and now he's chickening out. Fuck them both.

I don't know what I interrupted but I get the feeling it has something to do with me.

I eat dinner in the sitting room with one eye on the Fulham/Blackburn game on TV. Did you ever find yourself doing something and wonder why? I'm watching the game on TV and I'm finding myself thinking, this is shit. I'm shovelling forkfuls of roast beef into my mouth and my mind is wondering how the fuck Sky Sports gets away with this. I'm thinking how the match I saw this morning was better than this. All the glitz and all the razzmatazz is plastered on to dress up something with absolutely no substance or consequence. I keep eating and I keep watching. The remote is way over there.

Tuseday night after training I come home and there's a text on my phone. It's from Seán and it says **B in tmro.**

Twenty minutes after I get this text off of Seán there's a knock on our door. Our bell doesn't really work. I'm sitting in the kitchen eating my dinner and my Da shuffles off down the hall to answer it. His voice starts off real high and surprised but then dips down into a quiet rumble. The door closes and now somebody else is rumbling with him back towards the kitchen.

I stop eating with my fork halfway to my gaping mouth like something out of *Looney Toons* and I listen to the voices. The first is my Da's but the second is after covering me in a slick of sweat from one breath to the next. Instantly my heart rate has trebled.

Into the kitchen, into our woodchip and lino grotto filled with steam and the smells of fried onion, steps Dr Thorpe.

A half-chewed ball of cud falls out of my mouth and splats onto my plate.

In the yellow light Dr Thorpe's hair is glimmering like spider silk and his too-earnest face is wrapped around a perfect smile. Behind him, my Da is practically bowing.

I should do something but I am absolutely terrified. I am sixteen years old and am paralysed by fear. The yellow streak that I've always always had opens up and glues me to the seat. My mind is a frozen ball, locked solid.

Dr Thorpe goes, 'Hello there, little man. I just called round to make sure everything was alright after our little shock the other night.'

He can see I'm not moving. He can see that behind my eyes I'm basically shitting myself. And all the while there's this tiny little voice that's screaming way down in my chest that I have to say something. That I have to do something.

Dr Thorpe is smiling smiling smiling. And smiling he turns to my Da and smiling he puts a hand on his shoulder.

He goes, 'I hope we're all okay?'

Da nods and says, 'Ah, sure. We're getting by. The Galvin boy is being sorted out and our man there is fine once he's not in bad company.'

Our man.

I'm thinking, I'm not *our* anything.

Without being invited, Dr Thorpe sits down at the head of the table and he looks at me with this expression like something you'd see on daytime TV. Patronising and self-interested all at once. The expression of someone who is going to engage in a conversation but could not give two fucks about what anybody else says. It is an expression as shining and blank as the moon.

He fixes me with this expression and he says, 'You haven't had any more little episodes, now, have you? No more, *delusions*?'

The little voice in my chest, that brave little part of me, screams because my traitor head shakes mutely. I am terrified. Behind Dr Thorpe, Da is standing looking at me like I've just tracked shit across the carpet and between my legs my balls are trying to climb back up into my abdomen.

Dr Thorpe says, 'Good. Good stuff.'

Then he stands up and he turns to Da and he says, 'I hope you don't mind me calling around like this?'

And Da, like he's still middle-class, like he still exists in Dr Thorpe's frame of reference, goes, 'No bother at all, Doctor. You must be looking forward to the Strawberry Fair Golf Classic?'

Dr Thorpe's smile never moves and I'm wondering how the hell he keeps his face so static. It's like his flesh is as chemically bonded as his Pat Kenny hairdo. He is a man of oil and emptiness. And in him is something sour. If I listen really hard, I can hear it.

The dead meat smack of it.

To my Da he goes, 'I always look forward to it. Playing off ten this year and I've been getting in a little practice with my new rescue wood. Sweet as a nut, she is.'

Then there's a barb that my Da, the fucking bagel, completely misses. Dr Thorpe goes, 'I suppose you don't really get out to the club much in your present circumstances?'

Behind that question, behind the white wall of Dr Thorpe's teeth, I can hear silent laughter.

Da just shakes his head and goes, 'No. No, I don't. Not any-more.'

Dr Thorpe is nodding his head in pretend understanding and then he looks at his watch like an amateur dramatist and goes, 'Would you look at the time. Sure, I'd better be motoring. Loads more people to see. Are you sure you didn't mind me dropping by?'

Again, jaundiced under the naked bulb hanging from the kitchen ceiling, into the thick stink of fried offal and burnt veg-etables, my Da goes, 'No bother at all, Doctor.'

And Dr Thorpe goes, 'Splendid.'

And then he says something that makes me blink for the first time in what seems like days.

He says, 'Good man. And always remember. We're all in this. Understand?'

And just like that I'm six years old and standing in Dr Thorpe's kitchen again.

And then Dr Thorpe is gone.

The front door closes and I can breathe again and I can feel the sweat sticking my T-shirt to my back and trickling down like grease from my oxters. I'm breathing really hard but now instead of dragging in the clinging smells of cooking, it's like my lungs are sucking in something else. All at once my head is filled with a smell from ten years ago.

My sinuses are clogged with the pulpy sweetness of rose petals.

Seán's fading black eye is really noticable. In the hollow to the left of his nose and all across the heavy swell of his cheekbone there's this jaundiced stain. The flesh all around his eye-socket is still fairly puffy and the skin looks taut. Not one of the teachers asks how he came by it. Not one of the teachers asks how he came by it because if they do that, then he'd have to tell them and then things would get complicated. It's much better for everyone if they know what happened to Seán and that Seán knows that they know but no one does anything too official about it. I get the feeling though that if Seán strolled in one morning looking not much worse than he is right now then Mr Cowper would have Social Services calling out to his Da like a shot.

Mr Cowper is the school's Guidance Counsellor and his job seems mainly to consist of putting his arm around the shoulders of scumbags and telling them how special they are and how mean the world is. In recognition of this and all the other stuff that Mr Cowper does for them, the scumbags call him *Cowpat*. Occasionally though, Mr Cowper is pretty useful.

It's over a week now since I saw what I saw and the nightmares are still as bad as ever. The other stuff though, the sense of falling apart, the sense of the world about to swallow me, is starting to weaken. I did some research on it and the only thing I can put it down to is shock. It's like I was on the verge of a breakdown or something.

I'm glad Seán's back and I think he's glad to see me too. I have it in my head that we have to do something about Dr Thorpe. We have to prove to people that he's a murderer.

Two things are getting in the way of this.

Number one is the fact that when Seán comes back, he comes back on medication that has the same effect as really strong dope. It's like Seán's moving in a thick swaddling of fog. Now it takes whole, long minutes for anything you say to him to register.

Number two is the fact that the entire fucking school knows about the dead dogs. And I mean the *entire* fucking school.

The caretaker is the first one to open his mouth about them.

When you walk into the school you have to push open the doors to the main building and the Junior Resource Area. The outside of the building is all red brick and white plastic rainwater chutes and downpipes. The inside is all slick with linoleum and tile. The carpet was all replaced a year ago with this sort of plastic stuff that's supposed to be easy to clean. For *easy to clean* read *easy to scrape chewing gum off*. It's all polished and washed so that there's an oily sheen off every flat surface. The hallway, the stairs, the wire-reinforced glass of the doors, everything is industrial, institutional. Everything is pale green or the colour of sour milk. Think marrowfat peas. Along the skirting boards and streaked blackly on some of the floors, the marks of shoes and runners are indelible. The place smells like a hospital.

This one day when me and Seán walk in through the doors the caretaker goes, 'Oh, here they are. Lock up your labradors.'

Then he laughs like he's just told the funniest joke the world has ever heard.

I'm looking at him with his little square head set onto his non-existent neck and I'm going, 'Been reading a lot of Wilde lately?'

He blinks at me like I'm speaking a different language but it doesn't matter because the whole corridor is full of other people and they're all looking at me and Seán. Every face is an open sore of mockery and here and there little groups are starting to giggle and point.

Before Seán can start to moan I go, 'Let's just get to class.'

The first class is English and I'm sitting in my usual spot and trying not to think about how terrible my life has suddenly gotten. The classroom is the same marrowfat colour as the corridors outside and I'm sitting in this marrowfat cube and I'm trying to draw a picture to illustrate Montague's 'Killing The Pig'. Our English teacher, Mr Gorman, thinks that this helps us to *concrete-ise the abstractions*. I'm pretty sure that *concrete-ise* isn't a word.

There's a blank sheet of paper on the table in front of me and in front of the table is the whiteboard. Mr Gorman has his laptop hooked up to the digital projector and across the whiteboard images that Mr Gorman thinks might prompt us in the right direction are cycling one after the other. The digital projector hums and its colours bleed off the whiteboard onto the paper in front of me, washing it blue, washing it red, washing it yellow. I'm staring at the empty sheet with a pen in my hand trying to think as the projector's cycle begins and ends and stains my page with someone else's ideas. If you're at home, daytime TV does this same thing. *The Oprah Winfrey Show* comes on and now *Ally McBeal* comes on and now I find myself thinking about *Diagnosis Murder*. The All Singing, All Dancing Dick Van Dyke from *Mary Poppins* as a crime-solving genius doctor. Who'd have thunk it?

And now I'm wondering what Jessica Fletcher and Dr Sloane's kids would look like.

Colours are washing over my blank page and image after image slides onto the whiteboard, holds and then slides off again. The cycle begins and ends, begins and ends, and I must phase out for a bit because the knock on the classroom door startles me and I drop the pen. It rolls in a wounded arc and stops against a table leg. I haven't made so much as a mark on the page.

Mr Cowper walks in and is followed by a very very attractive lady. She's wearing a short black skirt that makes every single lad in the class do a cartoon double take, a white shirt, and she has dark hair framing a pale petal face. Her blue eyes look at me like she knows me. In her arms she carries a clipboard pressed to her chest. Now, like every other lad in the class, I'm staring and, like every other lad in the class, I'm suddenly envying a clip board.

Every other lad except Seán.

The medication that Seán's on has him completely zonked and he doesn't even notice that Mr Cowper and the lady have come in. He just sits there and in his big paw his pen is making a series of spirals on his page.

This morning I try to tell Seán that we can't just sit around and let Dr Thorpe get away with what he did. I try to tell him that we have to *do* something. We can't let a murder just happen.

Seán blinks at me really, really slowly and says, 'I don't want to.'

I shake him by the shoulders and his arms swing loose and heavy like tubes filled with water. I shake him by the shoulders and I go, 'For fuck's sake Seán, snap out of it. Stop taking those tablets. You're turning into a fucking zombie.'

Seán shakes his head and in the corridor other students walk around us. He blinks at me again and he goes, 'I'm not a monster. I like that.'

I'm looking at Seán now and I can see that in the centre of the page his concentric circles have gotten so close and so dense that he's almost put the ball point through the paper.

Then Mr Cowper's going, 'Sorry for disturbing your class, Mr Gorman, but could we have a word with the two lads please.'

He doesn't even say our names. Everyone knows exactly who he's talking about.

And now he's going, 'Bring your bags.'

I start to pack up my stuff but Seán just sits there with his pen swirling round and round on his page. The pen's making this low rumbling noise as it swirls around and around because Seán's resting way too much weight on it.

Mr Cowper's frowning at him and goes, 'Seán? Seán Galvin?'

Seán doesn't even blink and Mr Gorman leans over his desk and says, 'Earth to Seán. Is there anybody there?'

Seán looks up like he's in slow motion and the lady with Mr

Cowper takes a pen out of her shirt pocket and starts to write something down.

Behind me, all soft and slurred but pitched just loud enough so that everyone in the class can hear, someone goes, 'Woof.'

Mr Gorman's head snaps up but he can't make out who's said it because the whole class is now sniggering.

I can feel my face and neck going so red and so hot that it's actually, physically painful.

Seán is looking around him like he's just after waking up and Mr Gorman smiles down at him. There's a genuine expression of sadness and sympathy on his face and he says, 'Seán, would you like to go with Mr Cowper for a while?'

He says this like he's saying it to a four-year-old.

Seán looks around to see if I'm coming too and when he sees me with my bag on my back he nods slowly and goes, 'Okay. I like Mr Cowper.'

The rest of the class roars with laughter at this and some of the bigger dickheads are using the noise as an excuse to throw in a few more *woofs*.

At that moment I hate them all. I really, really hate them.

We, me and Seán, follow Mr Cowper and the lady outside and Mr Gorman closes the door behind us. Through it we can hear him letting loose at the lads. Mr Gorman's pretty sound and he's a good teacher but you don't want to cross him. He has this ability to make you feel ashamed of yourself and sorry for letting him down. It's a black magic that some teachers have. If you're not a teacher I think it's called *passive aggression*.

In the cold green and linoleum of the corridor Mr Cowper goes, 'Lads, this is Ms Herrity. She's from NEPS. Do you know what that is?'

Seán's just staring at Ms Herrity like he's never seen a woman before in his life and beside him I'm looking from her to Mr Cowper and back and I'm going, 'No. I'm sorry, sir. I don't.'

Ms Herrity is smiling this little crooked smile and she's saying, 'There's no need to be sorry. I'm from the National Educational Psychology Service. Your principal just wants me to have a word with you two gentlemen. Just to see how you're getting on.'

Seán doesn't say anything. The meds have thrown a lagging jacket around his brain and I've no idea if he realises that the very very attractive lady in front of us is a shrink.

Seán doesn't say anything but the words *you two gentlemen* have frightened me a bit. Seán is the fucked-up one. Not me. I'm grand.

Mr Cowper and Ms Herrity lead us up along the corridor that joins the Junior and Senior Resource Areas. On the walls photographs of previous classes are an archive of weird hairstyles and old uniforms. Mr Cowper's office is in the Senior Resource Area. His door is sandwiched between two banks of grey-painted lockers. You'd pass it without even knowing it was there. I know lads who went looking for it and couldn't find it. It's like the door to fucking Narnia or something.

At one end of the resource area the double doors to the school library stand closed with a sign on them that says, *Books trap the mind into thinking for itself.*

Mr Cowper's looking at me and then he puts an arm around my shoulders and then he's going, 'You just go and wait in the library for a while. We just want to have a quiet word with Seán for the moment.'

I'm watching as Ms Herrity guides Seán into the Guidance Office and now I'm shrugging and now I'm going, 'Okay, sir.'

The desks in the library are covered in a kind of slippery, hard veneer the no-colour of dust. Now I'm sitting at a no-colour study desk, a book unread at my elbow. The library is starting to fill up. The results of Mock exams and the approaching jugger-naut of the Leaving are starting to bleed the sixth years away from classes like Religion and P.E. They are clotted around library computers and study stations. You can tell the ones who are going to pass. They always look the most worried. It's a scientific rule that the outward calmness of the student is inversely proportion-al to the grade of the exam. It's always the harried, drawn ones that get As. There's a girl in a school jumper sitting at the desk in front of me. The cuffs of her sleeves are chewed into stringy net-ting. Beside her there's a leaning tower of books about to fall off the desktop and onto the slate carpet. She can't seem to take enough notes and her highlighter is wasting. I've never seen a highlighter waste before. Anyone who cares that much about her work can't possibly fail.

Then there's people like the two rugger buggers propping up the end of one row of books. They both play for the local rugby club and one is captain of the school team. The school team is rubbish but it's like they've read Ross O'Carroll Kelly without getting the irony. Both have the collars of their school polo shirts turned up and both are, like, screwed man, completely Daffy Ducked. I'm not underestimating them either. I know the one with the frost-tipped hair because he plays soccer too and, honest to God, he hasn't a clue. I don't care one way or the other about this but when he says, 'Oh yeah, English Paper Two's where I'll pick up the marks,' I nearly laugh.

The exams are just about two months away and if I were doing English Paper Two I wouldn't be worried.

I have never ever gotten less than 88 percent in English. It's what I do.

A few desks away from where I'm sitting there's another guy from football, Simon. He's sitting at a desk with his girlfriend. Simon's girlfriend is beautiful. I can't say it any better. I won't say anything else. The fact is she is just that. Beautiful. Simon's showing her off. He's sitting beside her with his arm draped around her shoulders like a hanging flap of something dead. A small group of friends crouch around their table and they whisper in dry leaf merriment. In the middle of the library.

I've heard that there's this college library in America somewhere that when it was built they forgot to factor in the weight of all the books so that when it was fully stocked the whole thing started to sink. According to the story it's still sinking. Year by year. Millimetre by millimetre. I'm pretty sure that story's a pile of crap but that's how I feel watching them.

I feel like I'm sinking.

I'm on my own here. Ignored by everyone and I don't know

what Ms Herrity and Mr Cowper are saying to Seán. I don't know why I'm being included in this. I haven't done anything wrong. It's like being friends with Seán is enough to make you catch whatever's wrong with him. It's like he's contagious.

I'm sitting at this table, my chin propped in the cradle of my palm, a book, unread, lying open before me like something on a dissecting table. The veneer of the desk is peeling at the corners and people have cut things into it over the years. The words 'cock' and 'fuck' feature prominently. This in a building full of books. On a two inch by one inch space someone's carved a straining penis and used a blue pen to ink its veins into a livid imitation of life.

I sit sinking at this mutilated desk and watch Simon and his girlfriend and their gaggle of friends.

She is the only girl amongst them. All the boys have a kind of spiky, tousled look to their hair. You take one fat slug of styling gel, one messy head and mix thoroughly. What you get is something hard and bristling. Like anger. *Her* hair falls in a wavy sheet. It is the colour of autumn. They all rustle with whispered laughter and the book remains unread at my elbow.

The library is policed by teachers who don't have a class right at the minute. They amble about with expressions of stupid, simmering fury on their faces. Simon's Da is the manager of the Bank of Ireland in town and you just know that the teachers have to keep in his good books.

One of these teachers walks up the aisle between the no-colour study desks. She's only young and this is her first year in here. She stops at Simon's little group and bends, telling them to be quiet or get out. They look past her and say, 'Yeah, okay, in a minute.' Her mouth opens, works silently, then closes and she walks on. Simon's group have already forgotten her.

Simon's head is on his girlfriend's shoulder and he lifts it at the new teacher's approach. Strands of her hair are caught on his artful spikes and remain strung between her head and his as the teacher talks and then walks. They scrawl across the air, red and alive like capillaries across skin.

I sit sinking and waiting.

Waiting for Mr Cowper to come and get me.

Waiting for Ms Herrity to say, 'It's okay, it's alright. It's not your fault.'

Me and Seán both went to the Christian Brothers Primary School in town. Looking back on it, those years were the happiest we've ever had. Both our Mams were still around. Seán hadn't really started to go off the rails yet. I still lived out beyond Cherry Orchard on the road out of town. We went to school. We did our homework. We played games. We were children. We were real-life, actual children. Not the in-between state we're in now.

The Brothers is this huge slab of a building, clad in pebble-dash the same chalky colour as bird droppings. Inside is all wood and wrought iron and the air of the place is a cold soup. With every breath you can taste the dust of ages past and when you run, the slick walls bounce back every footfall. The whole building chimes.

How it works is like this. On this side of town everybody, boys, girls, the whole shebang, goes to the Presentation. This is a mixed primary school run by the nuns. This is the place that Seán first started to preach the gospel of the Upturned Tayto Bag. Now, nobody tells you this but what happens is when you hit about seven years of age, at the end of First Class and after your First Holy Communion, Brother O'Neill comes to take all the boys to another school.

One day, towards the end of the year, Brother O'Neill arrives and every single First Class boy is lined up and taken to the Brothers. Until you hit about fourteen and start taking a serious interest in the opposite sex you won't see even half of the girls again.

How it happens is all the boys are called out of class and we line up in the yard. We line up in twos and we hold hands because that's the way you're taught to line up in the Presentaion. Brother O'Neill is all smiles and good humour and he's like that uncle that you only see at Christmas but who's full of craic and one-liners.

All of us chaps are all standing in line with our bags on our backs and we're all kind of nervous about heading off to the big boys' school. It's about a twenty minute walk away on our stubby little legs. Brother O'Neill walks us out of the Presentation yard in a double line of pale pudgy faces and pale pudgy hands linked to other pale pudgy hands.

When we're out of sight of the Presentation the first shock happens.

Brother O'Neill turns around and produces a ruler out of thin air. Then he walks back down our double line flicking his ruler at our clasped hands. He doesn't do this hard and he doesn't do it with any kind of venom or malice but he does it pointedly so that you get the message. One by one we all let go of our partner. Even Seán lets go of my hand before Brother O'Neill is anywhere near us.

When Brother O'Neill gets to the back of the line we're all turning around to look at him. Without a hand to hold on to some of the lads are sticking their fists into their mouths and drool is swagged in membranes over chins and fingers. We stand there clogging the entire footpath so that people have to walk in the gutter and others are stopping to stare at us in fond memory of their own sons taking this same trip. Year on year. Over and over again like some sort of annually migrating ant colony.

We're all watching Brother O'Neill and he puffs out his chest and he says in a voice that isn't loud at all but which has harmonics in it that cut through the traffic noise and the hubbub around us.

We're watching him and he goes, 'Ye're not babies anymore, lads. Ye're young men. Ye'll not hold hands like that again. By the time I'm done with ye, ye'll all learn how to stand on ye're own two feet.'

When he says this I remember thinking, this isn't like anything I've seen before. This teacher doesn't do that weird soft-voice thing. I remember thinking, he's speaking to us like he'd speak to anyone. And just like that I know I'm going to like the Brothers.

There's two of every class in the Brothers. Two Second Classes and two Third Classes all the way up to two Sixth Classes. No matter what anyone says, kids aren't stupid and it takes us about two days in the place to figure out that there's one smart class and one stupid class for every year.

Me and Seán are both in the smart class. I told you before that Seán isn't stupid.

One day when we're in Third Class we're all out playing Cops and Robbers. What happens is the two classes in the year all play together and at the start of lunch time we get a teacher to toss a coin and depending on who calls what, one class are the cops and the other class are the robbers.

The game's pretty cool and what you do is you catch the robbers if you're a cop and you make them stand in the shelter. The shelter is a huge concrete awning supported by reinforced concrete pillars with a wall at each end. It's built so that we have somewhere to stand if it rains. When you catch the robbers you stand them against the long back wall of the shelter with one of their arms extended out and their palm flat against the concrete. This is so that if one of the other robbers is quick enough and brave enough he can run underneath his friend's arm and free him from jail. And on and on it goes until everyone is caught and we do it all again tomorrow.

Describing it now it seems pretty lame but I bet if we did it for P.E. everyone would love it.

This one time we're playing Cops and Robbers and nearly all the robbers are caught. My class are the robbers this time and I'm standing there with my hand against the wall with the rest of my class waiting to be freed. I've been standing here now for nearly ten minutes and every minute another one of my class gets stuck against the wall. The cops, stupid class though they may be, have this all sewn up and they've set guards all along the arcade of the shelter. Still, I'm pretty confident that at least some of us will be set free because Freddie Masterson is still loose.

Freddie, with his blond hair and blue eyes, always always wins gold in the sports day hundred-metre sprints and he's like lightning on the hurling pitch. He does everything perfectly. The star of the school.

I'm watching the yard with everyone else. It's getting into October and little fists of spectators are knotted around conker matches and over the shrieks of the younger kids come the roars of 'Stamps!' and 'No fuckin' way! No stamps!'

Then, like a golden hare coursed by exhausted hounds, Freddie comes slaloming through the crowds. Behind him two lads from the stupid class are floundering like their feet are buried in mud.

We all straighten up because we know that Freddie's going to bob and weave and duck under our arms and set us free. He's running hard but not in the way you sometimes see children run, all pounding feet slapping off the cement, uncoordinated and slow. No, Freddie runs like a race-horse. His head is pushed forward and his limbs are strong and graceful. Even in Third Class he moves like an athlete.

The trouble is one of the cops sees him coming.

The trouble is one of the cops sees him coming and pretty accurately gauges that there's no way in hell he's got any chance of catching Freddie Masterson in full flight. Instead he just sticks out a leg and clips Freddie's ankles.

Freddie does a cartwheel. He's moving so fast that he actually leaves the ground and the clean lines of his elegance are replaced by this weird panicked flailing. I'm watching him do this kind of spastic fit in mid-air and then he hammers into the ground. His hands go out to try and save himself but it's too late and the noise of Freddie's face mashing into the concrete sounds wet and soft and solid all at the same time.

The dead meat smack of it.

When Freddie comes to a stop he leaves a red smear behind him. When Freddie comes to stop he leaves a red smear behind him and then he doesn't move. Everyone in the shelter is just watching him not moving and then he starts to cry. Then he's pushing himself off the ground and every sob he lets out sprays blood onto the backs of his hands and onto the hard, grey floor of the shelter. When he lifts his face you can see his nose is squashed flat and his broken teeth have torn his lips to shreds.

Brother O'Neill wants to know what happened.

I'm standing in front of his big wooden desk in his big wooden office and I'm looking at a leather that's been pointedly left in plain sight. It sits on the edge of the desk like the desiccated tongue of an unimaginable monster.

I'm only in Third Class but I've enough cop on to figure that Brother O'Neill would never use that thing in a bazillion years. All the stories of it though are winging around inside my head on little flittering rags of bat leather. All the stuff my Granda and my Da tell me to frighten me, telling me how they'd get a skelp of it just for getting a sum wrong. I know I'm never going to be on the receiving end of it but even so there's this sort of genetic memory associated with it. My eyes keep flicking to the leather and back to Brother O'Neill and I can see he notices.

Brother O'Neill goes, 'Who tripped him?'

My mouth is all dry and I can feel, actually *feel*, the leather cracking down across the backs of my hands. In spite of this though, I'm possessed of that boyish horror of ratting anybody out.

I'm weighing the likelihood of Brother O'Neill using the leather against the concrete fucking definite of the lads in the stupid class hammering the shite out of me for squealing and then I'm going, 'I don't know. I think he just tripped over himself. He was running really fast.'

Brother O'Neill is nodding to himself and then he says, 'That's what everyone says. Even the boy who tripped him.'

My mouth opens to say something but my brain catches up just in time and shuts it again.

Brother O'Neill's nodding and Brother O'Neill, still nodding, goes, 'Loyalty is an admirable trait. But I'd be careful about who you owe that loyalty to.'

Then he reaches for the leather and he lifts it off the desk and then I'm terrified and panicking and I get this horrible spasm in my abdomen. I'm going, 'Paddy tripped him. Paddy Courtney.'

Brother O'Neill pauses and his face opens up in an expression of pity and contempt. I can see that his other hand is about to open a drawer in his desk. And just like that I know he was putting the leather away. Not going to hit me. Not going to threaten me. Just stowing it away in its drawer.

I feel about two inches tall and Brother O'Neill is looking at me and like he's doing me a favour he goes, 'Don't worry. I won't tell anyone.'

I'm annoyed with myself. I'm appalled at the yellow streak that all of a sudden I know runs just beneath the surface of me. Standing there, sickened, I say, 'Thanks, sir. They'd kill me if they knew I squealed.'

Brother O'Neill is frowning now and he goes, 'No, I don't mean that. I mean . . .' and he points to my crotch.

There, against the dark grey of my trousers a darker charcoal is dappled. Just a few drops but enough to show that I've pissed myself.

And not caring about where I am and not caring that I'm only ten-years-old and not caring that this could get me into more trouble, at the top of my voice I'm going, '*Fuck!*'

I'm sitting in front of Mr Cowper and Ms Herrity and I might as well be back in Brother O'Neill's office. I'm watching them sitting behind the single no-colour desk and they're whispering to each other. Ms Herrity is taking notes in a hardback A4 copybook. I'm watching them and I'm hoping that whatever happens my yellow streak doesn't show through. I'm hoping that I'm not going to land Seán in trouble. I'm hoping that at least I can manage to not wet my pants this time.

They finish whispering and they both turn to me and smile like I can't see that they don't mean it. They're only smiling with the bottom half of their faces. Their smiles don't touch their eyes and I can see the little cogs and wheels spinning behind them.

Ms Herrity kicks things off by going, 'Tell us about your friend.' She then makes a show of rifling through her notes as though this isn't very important, like Seán's name isn't tattooed on the front of her brain.

She pauses and says, 'Seán Galvin.'

I look at her. I look at her pretty face and her tight blouse and I look at her pen poised above the A4 pad.

I look at her and I say, 'What do you want to know?'

She looks at Mr Cowper and Mr Cowper nods slightly and he says in this undertone that I'm meant to find reassuring, 'He's a good boy. I told you he'd want to help.'

Ms Herrity makes this little noise in the back of her throat that you could take as anything you like and then she's talking to me again. She's going, 'Tell us everything you can about Seán. Everything.'

I'm talking then but there's no way I'm going to land Seán in any more hot water. I'm talking but I'm being careful and my yellow streak is staying deep deep down. I tell them about the duck and about the dead dogs. But I don't tell them about Cha Whelan. I try to make Seán look as good as I can.

Then Ms Herrity is going, 'Tell us about this incident with Dr Thorpe. This was the night of the dead dogs, I believe. It's formed quite a jumble in Seán's head and he seems quite badly affected by the events of that night.'

Before I'm even conscious of it, my voice goes, 'I don't want to talk about it.'

Mr Cowper frowns and leans forward in his chair. He looks genuinely concerned and I figure this is what he must look like to all the scumbags who come in to make up excuses for acting the prick. All earnest and intense.

He goes, 'Why not.'

Something that feels like a python is coiling inside me, something torsional and muscular and cold. I'm swallowing now and it's like my mouth is filled with cinders. I'm swallowing now and I'm saying, 'Nobody believes us. They say we're making it up to hide what we were up to that night.'

Ms Herrity is smiling her plastic smile again and she says, 'We're not here to judge. We don't care what you were doing at Dr Thorpe's, and what Seán did with those dogs is really a cry for help. We're just here to make sure that Seán gets that help. He needs that help.'

Mr Cowper is nodding and grinning like she's just revealed the third secret of Fatima or something and then he's saying stuff. He's saying stuff that makes me want to smile. Remember when I said that, occasionally, Mr Cowper is pretty useful? Well this is one of those times.

Mr Cowper has his hands steepled together and he's looking over them at me and he's going, 'What kind of help do you, as

Seán's friend, think he needs? How can we build a network of supports for him? On his own terms? How can we facilitate his uniqueness as part of the wider school community? These are the questions we think you can help us with.'

I'm staring at him and he must see something in the way my face looks because he lifts his hands up as though he's Atlas hefting the world and he wiggles his fingers. He holds this pose for a moment and then he says, 'If this is frightening for you, think of yourself as a great oak tree. You are unshakable. You have deep roots.'

I'm looking from Mr Cowper to Ms Herrity, who at least has the good grace to look embarrassed, and I'm trying to stop myself laughing.

I'm looking from Mr Cowper to Ms Herrity and I go, 'I don't think Seán's tablets are helping him that much.'

Ms Herrity frowns and she scribbles something down and she asks, 'Even the new ones?'

I'm nodding and she's scribbling something else. Her pen makes these little skittering noises like there's a mouse behind the skirting boards.

I know this is the most selfish thing I've ever done but I can't do this on my own. I don't know what exactly it is that I'm going to do about Dr Thorpe but I know that I need Seán to do it. I'm going, 'They've taken something out of him. He's not Seán anymore.'

Then, because I know how Mr Cowper talks and thinks, I go, 'I feel that he's become powerless. He's become disenfranchised from himself. I feel, as his main support, that the tablets are simply allowing him to avoid the reality of his actions.'

Ms Herrity is looking at me like I'm a spaniel reciting Hamlet. She's frowning again and there's this cynical crook to her mouth.

She goes, 'Well, I'm sorry that you feel that way but Seán is staying on his medication. I understand how you feel but your friend has been assessed by professionals. Exhaustively assessed.'

But it's not Ms Herrity that I'm paying attention to.

Mr Cowper is leaning forward again and his hands are joined like he's praying or something. He has them pressed against his lips and his head is bobbing up and down and he's looking at me with this weird light in his eyes. There's an earnestness to him that's unnerving. What I've said has lit a fire in him. He's heard himself in me. He's heard himself and he likes it.

Mr Cowper has the same fervent expression that you see on the faces of fundamentalists everywhere. He believes in this crap. Believes it so much it seems like he's acting. Really *believes* in it. It's his creed and religion.

Ms Herrity however, is looking at him in the same way that most normal people look at fundamentalists.

Ms Herrity goes, 'Mr Cowper.'

Mr Cowper is still nodding and he's still looking at me like I've explained the meaning of life.

Ms Herrity goes again, 'Mr Cowper.'

And then she's going, 'Brendan.'

I'm taking this all in and I'm trying not to smile.

Mr Cowper shakes himself and he turns to Ms Herrity and he goes, 'You know, perhaps it is merely an exercise in smoke and mirrors to keep Seán medicated.'

He pauses and purses his lips and he doesn't notice that Ms Herrity exhales a little too sharply through her nostrils. And then he's going, 'Perhaps we are, in fact, *enabling* his dysfunction.'

Ms Herrity looks at Mr Cowper and then she throws me a look with broken glass in it. She puts her notepad and pen on the desk and she says, 'Mr Cowper. Seán Galvin should not be encouraged to withdraw from his medication without NEPS' or his doctor's intervention.'

I am a great oak tree.

And I'm going, 'It's just that he's sad all the time. Like Stephen Pepper.'

Mr Cowper is nodding again and his his face is all earnest behind his steepled fingers. Ms Herrity, however, is looking through her notes again and she gives me this weird crooked smile.

I smile back until she starts talking. Then the smile twists and dies on my face like something hit and mangled by a train. She's going, 'Have you ever attended counselling, yourself?'

Frowning now, I go, 'No. Definitely not. Why should I? I'm grand.'

Ms Herrity throws Mr Cowper a look that she doesn't even try to disguise. Mr Cowper sort of wriggles in his chair and I can hear the polyester of his trousers scrape on the plastic of his chair.

Ms Herrity's very very good-looking face then turns to me

and it's like someone's turned on a floodlight behind her eyes. She looks at me and it's like she's stripping every layer of veneer from me.

In the face of her hurricane beauty I blink and swallow and I try not to think of how full my bladder is.

She goes, 'There have been . . . ehm . . . incidents.'

I don't say anything and without once looking at her notes she goes, 'You were let go from a summer job for tampering with official documents in quite a, shall we say, graphic manner. Then there's this outrageous story you came up with up to protect Seán.'

Now I'm going, 'Wait a minute—' Ms Herrity, though, she just keeps right on talking.

'I have reports here from your Form Tutor and Year Head as well as some information provided by your fellow students. You seem rather outside of your own life. Disconnected.'

My mouth is so dry it's like my tongue is a piece of kindling. I'm swallowing hard and I'm going, 'What's that supposed to mean? What are you implying?'

Mr Cowper jumps in at this point and he says, 'Your circle of friends is quite . . . limited. And while your linguistic skills are remarkable your expression and outlook can be somewhat . . . ehm . . . I don't know. Surreal?'

At the same time as Mr Cowper says 'surreal', Ms Herrity says, 'Disturbed.'

They both look at each other and their overlapping voices have set up nasty harmonics in my head.

Now I'm looking from one to the other and I can hear, actually hear the fear and defensiveness in my voice. I'm going, 'No. Really. Really, really. I'm grand. Really.'

Mr Cowper looks at me and then looks down at his desk. Ms Herrity is writing again. Scritch-scritch. Scritch-scritch.

Nothing much else is said and when I'm leaving, Mr Cowper goes, 'We'll talk some more about this.'

I can see Ms Herrity is livid and when I close the door I can hear her start to give out.

At this stage there's only about twenty minutes of the last class of the day to go. I'm heading back through the Senior Resource Area and just as I'm about to turn down the corridor to the science labs, I see Seán sitting on a windowsill. There's only twenty minutes of the day left so I figure, fuck it. I walk over to him and sit down.

His face is blank as a field of snow and he doesn't even look at me. He just stares across the corridor, at a fly crawling up the far wall. I lean forward and try to catch his eye but he doesn't twitch a muscle. His eyes are dead balls of glass. I wave my hand in front of his face and a slow smile lifts his mouth in a shallow curve.

I stop waving my hand and I go, 'Shouldn't you be in Art?'

Still not looking at me, he says, 'There's only a few minutes left and I like it like this. It's all quiet. Nobody's looking at me or talking about me or anything.'

His voice isn't like it used to be. It sounds like a recording.

I go, 'Nobody's talking about you, Seán.'

This is bullshit but I have to say something.

Seán goes, 'What did Mr Cowper want to talk to you for?'

I'm looking at Seán and now I'm frowning and now I'm going, 'He was wondering what we have to do to help you.'

Seán nods slowly and then he says, 'We forget all about the dead dogs. We forget all about Dr Thorpe. We take our tablets and we're just like everyone else. I don't want anybody to look at me. I don't want anybody to talk about me.'

Then something breaks in me and I can feel wet on my face even though I don't feel like crying. Even though I don't feel like crying there's tears coming out of my eyes and my lips are all in spasm.

I can hear my voice going, 'I can't forget, Seán. You didn't see what I saw. You didn't hear it. We have to do something.'

I'm dragging my sleeve across my face and it comes away messed with snot and spit and saltwater. When it comes away I can see Seán staring at me. There's a light in his eyes again for the first time in what seems like forever.

He looks at me for a long time and then he's saying, 'Why are you crying?'

I'm sniffing and I'm trying to stop myself crying and I go, 'Because I can't do anything on my own. Because those tablets you're on have you zonked.'

Seán turns away and faces the far wall again and he's quiet for a minute and then he says, 'Maybe I can talk to Mr Cowper. Maybe he can help me with my tablets or something.'

Joe Murphy

And like Judas himself, weak-willed and selfish and conniving, I go, 'Yeah. Maybe that'd be a good idea.'

I told you. I'm not a nice guy, sometimes.

It's strange how people latch on to someone they see as stronger than themselves. When you get right down to it any relationship is an unequal partnership. Strip away all the peripherals, all the pink fluff and you're left with one person who wants and another who needs. This is true for relationships of more than two people as well. Long chains of interdependence. Long chains of people who are so dysfunctional they'll allow themselves to be kicked around rather than face rejection, rather than force a confrontation. Rather than cause a fuss.

Hello, my name is John, my name is Mary, my name is James, and I'm a football.

If this were a third world country there'd be a revolution. Instead we watch as money is siphoned off, misappropriated, misused. We watch from an unmoving line of cars and listen to the girl on the radio announcing a slight increase in employment. We listen and we know for a fact that this is bullshit because three factories back home just shut down. Whole villages are left scratching their heads and wondering who buys the D-reg mercs that own the roads. Sleek and arrogant. We sit and shrug and watch the taillights paint the world red.

If life is a seesaw then its fulcrum is always askew.

And now I'm wondering, am *I* any good? Is my fulcrum askew?

People are strange.

We sit in silence as the day slouches towards the final bell. There's noise in the corridor before the bell because a lot of teachers let classes out early so they can get to their lockers and the buses and stuff. Me and Seán are just sitting there on the windowsill and all these people are streaming past us.

Then Benny Mythen comes along on all fours and barks at us before standing up again and running off down the corridor barking and yelping. Half the school sees this and half the school is creased up laughing at the two of us.

I'm pissed off at this but beside me Seán's head has dropped below the level of his shoulders and his whole body is dissolving into a swamp of sobs. Under his breath I can hear him going, 'I'm sorry. I'm sorry. I did a bad thing. I don't want to do it again. Never again. Never ever.'

Before I know what I'm doing, I'm putting my arm around his shoulders and everyone goes, 'OOOOOOoooooooohhhhhhh.'

Someone I can't see shouts, 'Faggots!'

Then people scatter because Mr Byrne, the Vice Principal, comes along. In his heavy voice he's saying, 'Break it up here. The bell's gone. Haven't you any homes to go to?'

When he sees me and Seán, he stops and plants his hands on his hips and he breathes air out through his nose so hard that I can hear it over the noise of everyone else.

He looks down at the sobbing Seán and he goes, 'I should have known I'd find you two in the middle of this.'

And then he goes, 'You've had it ruff over the past while, haven't you, Seán?'

I'm sure he means *rough* but what I hear is *ruff*.

He throws his eyes over the two of us, me with my running nose and red lacing my eyeballs, Seán with his head down, crying softly, my arm around his shoulders. He takes all this in and he goes, 'Look after each other, lads. Remember who your friends are.'

Then he goes, 'I'll get Mr Cowper.'

And way back in my hindbrain I can hear Judas start to giggle.

I've known Seán Galvin for a long time but that hateful traitor that lives in the back of my head is a more recent acquaintance. I figure he gets louder the older you get and the more reasons you have to fuck other people over. The first time he yammered at me was last Halloween when I fucked off and ran leaving Seán pretty much high and dry in one of the weirdest happenings of my entire life.

The Halloween Holidays rock around and me and Rory and Seán are all allowed to go up to Dublin because Tim Minchin is doing a gig. I love Tim Minchin and I've been trying to get Rory into him so we can all stay in his brother Davey's college res flat. We all get permission to stay up for a whole week, an entire seven days, and Davey's actually being pretty sound about this and he says there's absolutely no problem with the three of us staying in his.

Rory and Davey's parents don't know that their eldest son has pretty much quit college. Neither does the college, so he's still living in the solid cube of unvoiced rancour that is his res flat. The atmosphere is lifted somewhat by virtue of the fact that his flatmate has, more or less, upped sticks and left. I don't know where he's gone but he's never, ever there when we are and most of his food is gone from the fridge. This is a good thing because we can fit more cans in the lower bit now and more food in the freezer compartment. He also never took the TV, which Davey says is his, so I presume he's about somewhere. The downside of him leaving is the fact that Davey says he used to have lots of good-looking-in-a-children-of-the-damned-type-way gal pals. And now, since his flatmate left, there are no more ash blonde female clones around the place. Irritating but fun to look at.

Our first day there Davey tells me he's running a courier business. Current staff: Him. Current assets: His Peugeot. Name: mercury.com. Davey doesn't have a computer nor does his crappy courier service have a website. Everything is a dot.com now. He even has a slogan, *Because Life Doesn't Wait*.

I ask him what that's supposed to mean. He says, 'Whatever.'

People take a thing that doesn't mean anything and make it mean whatever they want. You take something trite, something vapid and suddenly it's a life choice, a philosophy. Davey does this. He screws people over. People ring his number, ring mercury.com, because life doesn't wait, so they can get a package from point A to point B and what they actually get is Davey and his Peugeot.

I ask him how many customers he gets. He says, 'A few.'

I'm laughing again now. At him this time. Seán and Rory are

arguing over the remote and I'm standing in the kitchen talking to Davey. His black hair is combed through with Brylcreem so that it lies furrowed and sleek and his tar pit eyes are oval holes.

Now he's looking at me and the holes of his eyes seem to drink in all the light and he goes, 'It's a start-up venture. It's a crappy job but at least it's honest. It's real work. It beats the shit out of this concrete mess full of hypocrites and posers.'

This I have to admit is true.

Then he goes, 'Or do you want to watch your soul shrivel up in an office somewhere? Like last summer? Since you're here, do you fancy lending a hand? Rory says you're pretty hot-shit with words.'

Nothing good will come of this. I say, 'I'll think about it.'

The afternoon after the Tim Minchin gig, Rory and Davey go out to get more cans and I'm on my own with Seán. I sit in the bleach glare of Davey's flatmate's TV and make up flyers for Davey's company. Because life doesn't wait.

Davey's parents are anxiously awaiting the 2.1 that he'll get in his finals. They're over two months away and his Mam wants him to send out CVs already. As I said, they don't know that he's quit college. It would break their hearts. He has stopped taking their money though. His Da's a bit suspicious about this but Davey says he's starting to make a bit of cash and he'd feel bad taking their money under false pretences. Now when I say *a bit* I do mean *a bit*. The point is he's making it.

The company works like this. There's the legitimate business that Davey says is useful for cover. Then there's the stuff Davey never told anyone, except Rory, about before. This is where he makes his money. This is how he can afford to buy Rory every Xbox game under the sun.

It turns out that Davey has an unsurprisingly large number of unsavoury friends. Said friends seem to want a lot of packages delivered to a lot of people with the minimum amount of fuss. For this Davey's friends pay him large amounts of money, which he then puts back into his joke of a Peugeot or uses it to buy other extravagances. Like proper food.

However, Davey's unsavoury friends and the people to whom they're sending large padded packages tend to be a bit unpredictable. In Davey's words they're prone to *throwing the bottle out of the pram*. In anyone else's words, they're prone to *shooting each other*. This is not an ideal state of affairs for Davey; which is where I come in.

mercury.com wants more normal people to use it so Davey won't have to drop brown paper parcels to large men on bleak housing estates. Davey's head is full of big ideas. He wants me to make up flyers, he wants me to set up an actual, real-life web page, he wants me to ignore the voice in my head screaming that this is fucking nuts. So I do and I make flyers and start designing web pages and try to snap free of teenaged sensibilities. I am not some docile, slaughterhouse animal. I am not a gap to be filled.

Davey's folks haven't seen him for three months now. This doesn't worry them. Sometimes nobody sees or hears from Davey for a lot longer. Usually when this happens he's associating with his unsavoury friends. Usually when this happens he comes back with a roll of notes that keeps him going for a couple of weeks. It doesn't bother me that Davey, and by extension, I, are working for criminals. Civil servants, bank clerks, they all work for criminals too. The only difference being that politicians and the heads of financial institutions never do business in the shadows cast by a burning car. As rationalisations go this is better than nothing.

Davey won't change the slogan. I'm annoyed by this. The fact that I'm going to spend the guts of a week making and photocopying hundreds of flyers with the words *Because Life Doesn't Wait* slanted across them irritates me. I tell him that it doesn't mean anything and he tells me that Feng Shui's a pile of crap too but people bought into that. People don't want substance, they want something as empty as they are. They want something so blank they can project anything they like onto it. The slogan stays and for the next four days I photocopy and drop through letterboxes dozens of flyers which most people ignore but some actually read.

As Davey said, business is starting to pick up.

Davey says he now has two best jeans and three nicest shirts.

He has a bank on his books now. Davey knows someone in marketing who needs to get a bag full of signed documents over to his assurance guys every day before twelve noon.

See also Declaration A.

See also Declaration B.

See also Direct Debit Mandates.

This, as far as I'm concerned, is regular and above board

income. When I say this to Davey he looks at me and smiles around his mouthful of teeth and says it's a means to an end. And I'm wondering, an end to what?

I'm sitting in the Ikea-minimalist cube that is his flat and his fridge is empty of food. The flat is empty of anyone else. Seán and the boys have gone to get Subway. The place is weirdly quiet without them. No one except Davey's friends ever calls here anymore and he uses the empty bedroom to store paper and boxes. On my own I keep the TV turned on and up so that its light reflects off everything and I can even hear it in the toilet. Apart from this I'm alone.

I'm trying to design a new flyer for mercury.com. There's a blank sheet of paper on the table in front of me and in front of the table is the TV. On the TV Jessica Fletcher is about to bury her saggy old woman's head into another murder mystery. There's this scene in *The Lost Boys* where the family drive by a billboard. The front of this billboard is plastered with a generic, *Welcome to . . .* poster. On the back though some local yokel has spray-painted the words *Murder Capital of America*. I'm watching Jessica Fletcher potter about the backwoods of Cabbott Cove and I'm thinking, fuck that, Maine is the Murder Capital of America. Still Jessica's got her head screwed on. I'm thinking that local sheriff couldn't find his own arse with both hands and an atlas.

Colours are washing over my blank page and programme after programme begins and ends, begins and ends, and I must phase out for a bit because Davey rattling his key in the lock startles me.

He walks in and is followed by a very very attractive girl. She's wearing a short denim skirt, a poncho and she has dark hair framing a pale oval face. Her blue eyes look at me like she knows me. Now I'm staring and now I'm wondering why no one else is spending time alone with a blank sheet of paper and now Davey's grinning at me. He's grinning and saying, 'Mind if we disturb you? We're just going into my room for a bit.'

Before I can say anything back the strange girl's going, 'Is *The Vampire Diaries* on yet?'

I'm still staring and I'm saying, 'It doesn't have all the channels.'

Then Davey's leading her by the hand. Then Davey's leading her into his bedroom and he's saying, 'Bet you're glad you stayed the week. And doesn't this beat the shit out of that office job you had?' Then Davey's shutting the door. He never even waits for my answer.

I'm thinking this is exactly like that fucking office job.

Getting sacked from the insurance place isn't the worst thing that's ever happened to me.

The blank page in front of me remains blank and the TV floods with people who make a noise that sounds like language until you realise that they don't communicate anything. Once you realise this you stop listening. I'm thinking that when a crime-solving pensioner constitutes cutting-edge viewing then we're in trouble. My page turns blue, turns red, turns yellow and stays empty.

The page stays like this until the bedroom door opens and the very very attractive girl walks out. Then the bedroom door's swinging shut and then she's opening the front door and then she's leaving without saying a word. She has a bruise on her neck. It is the colour of storms.

I'm wondering, would she have stayed if we had all the channels?

I'm wondering how this page is still blank. My inevitable A in English should mean that I have an ability to conjure something that at least sounds good from absolutely nothing. Shazam. Sitting here, staring at nothing, I'm starting to doubt my amazing talents. Davey's amazing talents are beyond any kind of doubt. mercury.com is making money for him and Davey's unsavoury friends are paying him shitloads of cash to keep ferrying plain brown packets around the place. Davey and his Peugeot never seem to stop and Davey's luck with girls is making me sick. The TV shivers from picture to picture and on his bed Davey's pulling up his trousers. I can hear his belt buckle and keys rattling like a charity bucket half empty of change.

My thoughts feel congealed. They are stuck to the inside of my skull, sluggish and viscous. Like phlegm.

I'm starting to get annoyed with myself and I'm more than a little surprised when Davey comes out of my bedroom and starts talking to me. I look at him blankly for a minute. His face is flushed and his hair is oily with sweat and it's seeping in lines down his forehead and into his eyes. I blink once. I blink twice. To me Davey sounds like one of the adults from *Snoopy*. Wah wahwah-wah wah.

I think he notices I'm not getting this. He's grinning his sickle grin and he's repeating himself. He's going, 'Do you want to head on the road? You look a bit stressed. The boys are coming too. They're meeting us downstairs. Your mate Seán's alright. A bit weird but alright.'

This is the nicest thing I've ever heard him say.

I say, 'Sure. Where're we going?'

His grin is widening and it's starting to look like a segment has been chopped out of his face. He's tapping the side of his nose with one finger and he's going, 'We've a job to do.' Then he's going, 'No rest for the wicked.'

This isn't an answer but I know it's all I'm going to get. I take a look at my empty page. It looks soured in the light thrown back off the curdled milk walls. I'm looking at this page and I'm crumpling it up and I'm turning off the TV. I want out of the res bloc and I need to get rid of the sticky feeling inside my skull. It's like I need to rinse out my brain somehow.

Davey's joke of a Peugeot is parked outside in the drizzle.

I don't know how old the car is but its number plates have a lot of Zs and Xs and the rear one is red. I'm no expert but I'd guess it's older than Davey. It's sitting there in the drizzle and water is gathering on its roof, gathering on its windows, gathering on its bonnet. Davey's Peugeot is red. Not the red of valentines or the slick oily red of a promo picture. It is the red of a scab and it sits on the tarmac, ragged and flaking as a scab. Rust is chewing the wheel arches to honeycomb and the red paint is blistered up around the edges of the handles and the moulding of the windows. As I said,

I'm no expert but I'd guess it wouldn't pass the NCT.

Rory and Seán are standing beside the car and when Seán sees me he grins this little child's grin and waves at me. It'd be embarrassing if you didn't know him.

Right now all round me and Seán and Rory and Davey people are looking out their windows. Their faces are pale masks stuck to the wet glass. Behind them the anaemic flicker of television plays like dull lightning.

Davey's grinning is a shark's head and he's saying, 'Fucking sheep.'

And now I'm wondering, are we as alien to them as they are to us?

Davey's getting into the Peugeot and then he's leaning across the passenger side and then he's swinging open the door. Over the arthritic groan of the hinges he goes, 'Hop in and lets blow this popsicle stand.'

Davey pops the locks on the rear doors. Seán and Rory are giving out about Xbox vs Playstation and they clamber in the back. I'm getting into the passenger seat and then I'm closing the door.

Davey drives out of college and onto the Clonskeagh Road. The drizzle's stopping and the traffic's moving and I'm glad to be out of the flat. The interior of the car is cluttered and does not smell like fake pine. I'm looking around and then Rory's asking, 'Where *are* we going?'

Davey winks at me and starts to whistle. He's whistling that song from *The Italian Job*. This doesn't fill me with confidence.

And now I'm saying, 'That doesn't fill me with confidence.'

The drizzle has left pearls of water all around the edges of the windscreen and with the forward motion of the car they are elongating and flowing upwards against the slope of the glass. It's like they're defying gravity.

Ranelagh is a solid mess of parked buses and oversized 4x4s are trying to nose their way out of side streets. I'm watching a suburban housewife with inevitable blonde hair try to insert a silver BMW X5 into a gap that you couldn't wedge an After Eight into. She sits there gunning the engine and rocking the beemer forward and back. Her blonde bob is flaring out as she twists her head left and right and there's a look about her of someone whose self-regarding bustle has been baulked by mere plebs.

A gap opens up but Davey slides the Peugeot into it. Slick as eels.

I'm looking at the woman in her beemer and it's like she's going to scream.

In front of us a bus is parked so that it blocks traffic. There's a tangle of people trying to get on at the same time as half the bus is trying to get off. Between us and the bus a guy on a bicycle is having an argument with a taxi driver. Above us the sun is coming out.

Davey's joke of a Peugeot doesn't have a radio let alone a CD player. We sit more or less in silence until we get to town. Then Davey goes, 'We're going to Capel Street.'

This strikes me as a bit odd and I'm saying, 'Why Capel Street?'

Davey's indicating and then he's changing his mind and then someone's leaning on their horn. Davey ignores this and he's saying to me, 'We've a package to pick up. Interesting this one. You'll love it.'

Not paying any attention to the road he turns around in his seat and he grins at Seán and Rory and says, 'You'll all love it.'

Rory frowns at his big brother and Seán just grins back. He likes it when people smile at him.

I don't entirely believe Davey and I'm turning to take in his profile as he drives. He has that habitual look of smugness that hints at the arrogance underneath and I'm asking, 'Is this legitimate income?'

Davey's grinning in his predatory way of grinning and he's going, 'This is.' Then he turns and jabs his thumb over his shoulder, 'That isn't.'

Now I'm turning and the seatbelt bites into the slack bulge of flesh beneath my lower ribs. In the footwell behind the driver's seat, between Seán's big feet, there's a parcel wrapped in brown paper.

I look at Davey and I look at the parcel and then I look at Davey again. His grin is fixed in place and I can feel the laughter coming from his wellhead eyes. Feel. Not hear. He says nothing and not a sound slips from between his lips but I can feel him laughing. Deep down and hidden.

I'm not going to ask what it is. I know that if I do he'll just grin or tap his nose or start whistling something. So I'm turning back around and I'm feeling the seatbelt loosen its grip.

Davey parks the Peugeot in an alley just off Capel Street. There's a billboard high up on one wall so that it can be seen from the main street. On it the corrugated torsos of American wrestling stars look cold and hard as concrete. Their faces gurn and the tendons of their necks look like cables. I know for a fact that they wouldn't last five minutes in the company of Davey's friends. You take one brash yank with tumescent pecs and balls shrunken to the size of peanuts and mix thoroughly with a gang of drug dealers. What you get is a bloody mess and a gang of drug dealers looking to buy an oversize coffin.

Around the corner from where Davey parks his car there is a sex shop. This is where we are going. Davey stops outside it and me and Seán and Rory stand there looking uncomfortable. We stand there for a minute and I say, 'You're joking.'

The building is like the one Rory's family lives in back home. Above ground it is a stacked hodgepodge of unreliable-looking electric shops and unused flats. In most of the windows grime is making dirty sweeps across the glass like the fake snow of forgotten Christmases. I'm wondering could anyone ever live in those rooms again. I'm wondering how long it would take to get rid of the stink of decay. Every window is a welling eye.

At ground level the spikes of a guardrail spring out from the building's front. In front of us though there's a low gate with steps leading down to the basement. The basement windows look out onto this stairway except they're all blacked out and a necklace of purple neon gives them a garish border. Above the basement door the sign says FUNTASY. And I'm saying, 'This is legitimate?'

Davey's looking at me and I'm thinking that he's thinking I'm such a soft chap. Then Davey's going, 'Come on, you pack of pussies.' Then Davey's going down the steps and we all follow in his wake. We are all children. We are all puppies on a string.

We stop at the bottom of the steps and Davey says, 'Press that buzzer over there.'

There's a button in the shape of a heart set into a speaker set into the doorframe. Rory's pressing it before I even get the chance to question why. A man's voice crackles out from the speaker and it's saying stuff. It's saying stuff like, 'Have you got an appointment? Or order number?'

Davey's grinning again and now his teeth are reminding me of the spiked railings overhead. And now Rory's going, 'Ehm . . . this is mercury.com.' He doesn't know what else to say.

The voice says, 'Jaysus Davey, is that you? Come in come in. I have it waiting for you here.' Then there's a sound like a dentist's drill and the door's lock snaps open and me and Seán and Rory and Davey push our way into the basement. For some reason my brain refuses to think of it as a sex shop. It is the basement. It is not FUNTASY.

The basement's interior is dark and I can't see anything for a minute. My irises expand and contract and I'm starting to realise that we're in a kind of hallway. The door swings shut behind us and we are all suddenly lit only by a single pink bulb. There's a beaded curtain in front of us and between its rattling fronds fluorescent brilliance is sharply filtered. The overall impression I'm getting is of sheer class.

Then Davey's slipping his way through the curtain and we're following. Lately I seem to spend the majority of my life following people. The room we're in is fucking huge. Aisle upon aisle of shelf upon shelf of weirdness fills it from wall to wall. Davey's walking down the middle aisle and we're following him past vibrators. Following him past handcuffs. Following him past ball gags. Following him past butt plugs. Following him past the hugest collection of kinky videos that I've ever seen. There's a counter at the end of the aisle and behind the counter there's a middle-aged man with a bald head emerging like a turtle's from a very expensive-looking suit. Apart from us and Davey and the man behind the counter there's no one else here. Beside the counter there's a mannequin dressed in a studded leather gimp suit complete with buckled hood. The metal stitching of a zip is drawn closed where the mouth should be and reminds me in a fucked up way of Zippy from *Rainbow*. The price tag attached to the mannequin's wrist reads €5000. I'm thinking being a pervert must be an expensive hobby.

Yer man behind the counter is looking at us with one eyebrow cocked. The light is reflecting off the smooth hairlessness of his head and the loose skin of his neck rasps against his shirt as he looks at Davey and three sixteen-year-old boys. The shirt looks silk and where the line of his collar meets his neck it has discoloured from the acids in his sweat. He's looking at us, at me and Davey, and then he says, 'mercury.com? Why the fuck did you call yourself that?'

And I know what Davey is going to say before he says it. He says, 'Because life doesn't wait.'

Now the man behind the counter is laughing and now he's bending down and he's taking a brown parcel from under the counter. It is exactly the same as the one lying in the Peugeot's footwell. Then he's reaching inside his inside pocket then he's taking out a tightly rolled wad of twenties and then he's peeling off six of them. He places them on the packet and slides the whole lot across the counter. Now he's looking at us and he starts off saying one word, 'Discretion.'

Our oddball meeting ends very quickly after this and the upshot of it is that we have to deliver this package to a very large house in Drumcondra whose resident is also very large and very well respected. Hence the discretion.

The basement door clicks shut behind us and the locking mechanism grinds angrily to itself. The outside is bright after the basement and I can't see anything for a minute. My irises expand and contract and I'm starting to realise that I've been left holding the package. I ask Davey how come I'm carrying the fucking thing.

He tells me that he's the one driving so I do the carrying. It's like we're married.

Davey's joke of a Peugeot is still parked in the side alley. There's a little runt of an inner city scumbag sitting on the bonnet. He couldn't be any more than twelve but already he's developing that inner city Dublin thing. That weird permanent shadow on the upper lip. That weird thing that never really turns into a proper moustache but remains marked and indelible as a permanent marker. The twelve-year-old with the knacker 'tache isn't alone and a tiny red-headed boy kitted out in a Kappa tracksuit and white runners emerges from behind the car. He is tucking his penis away and I'm hoping he didn't take a slash against any of the door handles. For some reason I'm nauseated by the sight of them. By the sight of their leering mouths, their aggressive little bodies, their little faces so pugnacious and brazen.

A mate of mine down home used to have this theory about Dublin kids. He saw them as some virulent kind of weed growing in the lightless spaces between tenements and office blocks. He figured that if you deprive a plant of light and proper nourishment it becomes pale and limp and stunted.

Standing here in this alley looking at the two kids in front of us, I'm willing to concede he may have had a point.

Davey's looking at the two young fellas and his black black eyes make him look ready to do murder. His mouthful of teeth turns into a maw and he's roaring at the two kids in front of us. I can see the anger in him. I can feel the violence coming off him in waves.

When he moves, he moves like lightning.

Young knacker 'tache is sliding off the bonnet and his belligerent little head is puckering around a frown. The frown lasts about two seconds. Davey's right arm snaps out and I'm blinking at the ferocity in it. The alleyway seems to shrink and all lines of perspective are now leading to the blood spurting from knacker 'tache's nose. I can't take my eyes off it.

The sound that Davey's fist makes as it connects with the cartilage and flesh of the kid's nose is something that months later

I'll hear again. The smack of it as it ruptures blood vessels. The dead meat smack of it.

Young knacker 'tache is down on the ground. He holds his nose and starts to cry. His red-head companion is trying to dart around Davey and he's yelling, 'I'm telling me Da!'

Davey grabs him on the way by and now he's pinning him to the wall. His eyes are fixed on the young fella's face and he's going, 'If you tell anyone. Your Da. Your Ma. Anyone. They'll never find your body.'

Little red-head goes quiet, goes limp, goes still. I'm thinking that if he hadn't just taken a whiz he'd be pissing himself by now.

Now Davey's dropping him and the young fella goes over to his bleeding friend. Both of them are crying now. Both of them are terrified. Their faces are pale as paper.

Beside me, Seán has his face in his hands and he's starting to moan.

When the kids leave Rory and Seán and Davey all go to get back into the car.

Not me though. I stand looking in at Davey with the glossy furrows of his hair raked across his skull. Davey looks at me and through the driver's side window, he goes, 'What? What's wrong with you?'

I don't say anything and I take a sort of half-step backward.

Inside the car, Seán's big face is swivelled to stare at me and with his heavy jowls and wide dull eyes he looks like a puppy behind dog-pound glass. He's about an inch away from putting his paws against the window.

I don't really want to get back into the car.

I don't want to get back in but I don't want to leave Seán either. Leave him with Davey sitting behind the wheel and his white face turned towards me. His eyes are so dark they look gone. It's like the crows have been at him. He sees me seeing him and he doesn't move and his eyes seem like mineshafts and in my head I can hear his fist connecting with my own gormless face. The dead meat smack of it.

It is now, right now, that the little Judas who lives in the back of my head first starts to squawk. I don't know how long he's been in there. I don't know how long he's been battening on the soft stuff of my brains but when he starts squawking he doesn't stop.

Little Judas is going, *Seán's a fucking looper. Leave him ta fuck here and get your arse back home. Davey won't be happy if anything goes wrong. Davey's fucking dangerous. You're afraid of Davey, aren't you? Seán can look after himself.*

I am the worst friend ever.

Along with Judas this is the first time I'm realising that I have no real friends, that I have no life outside of Seán and what we do together. Football is well and good but Rory's really the only one I get on with and I'm not sure if I want to get on with him anymore. I'm realising this and I nearly drop the package.

Without really knowing what I'm doing I go to take another half-step backward.

Davey looks at me and then he looks at the package in my hands. And then, smiling, he looks over his shoulder into the back of the car. Seán is frowning at me but not in an angry way.

There are tears in eyes. Actual honest-to-God tears. He doesn't understand why I'm leaving him.

Davey, still smiling, turns back to me. And then in the car both Davey and Rory start to laugh and Davey's going, 'You're some boy, aren't you? You cowardly little rat.'

This is the plain truth of things. Truth is not glazed earthenware. Truth is not silk-smooth sandalwood. Truth is a heavy thing of rust and ragged edges.

In my head Judas is screaming with laughter like the sound of scrap being compressed.

I look at Davey and the violence in him is a thing of little snagging hooks. I look at Davey and then I look at Seán's soft face and then, trying not to think too hard about it, I get back into the car.

In the back beside Seán, Rory's face looks like it's had all the bones removed. Seán is smiling like a baby with wind. His face is all contorted and his lips are wriggling wide with happiness. I am disgusted with myself.

I toss the package behind the driver's seat. I am on automatic. The whole ugly little incident reminds me of what's been under the surface with Davey. It reminds me of how fucked up the guy is. It reminds me that I'm scared of him.

And then, off-hand like he's talking about football results, Davey's going, 'That'll teach the little bastards to fuck with someone's car.'

I'm wanting to tell him that they didn't do anything. I'm wanting to tell him they were only kids. I'm wanting to tell him to let me out of the car. I'm wanting to get out of the car and leave all this behind me. All this. Everything. Right now, Seán is a yoke about my neck and the guilt that I'm feeling hurts my stomach.

But I don't do anything. Instead I sit there in silence as Davey eases the Peugeot out into traffic.

Dorset Street and the Drumcondra Road are pretty okay traffic-wise. It's hard to believe but it's still only mid-afternoon. The car is silent. The tension is palpable. It seems to fill all the available space. When you inhale it leaves a copper tang at the back of the throat. I'm trying not to remember the child's cracked face but I can't help it.

Seán is still moaning softly to himself like the sound of distant sirens.

We're stopped at the traffic lights beside Fagan's and Davey finally says, 'Alright. Maybe I shouldn't have hit him.'

Rory goes, 'Yeah.'

And just like that I'm thinking, well at least he knows he was wrong. And just like that we're all papering over the cracks again.

After this, Judas start to talk to me a lot. But after this, as well, I know that I'll never cut and run on Seán again, no matter what Judas says. And here I am trying to get Seán to stop his medication because I haven't the balls to do anything on my own.

The yellow in me is enough to paint the world.

Derek Meyler, our next-door neighbour, smokes about sixty Sweet Afton a day. Because of this he has this wheeze that you can hear a mile off. This is why I don't jump when he leans over the concrete wall between our back yards and goes, 'How's it goin', chap?'

I'm in our back yard hanging out the washing on the length of twine that passes for our washing line. I'm taking my time about it though because the atmosphere in the house is crawling. When I sit down it's like there's things with little scuttling legs moving all over me. So I'm out here in the yard now for maybe half an hour.

It's pretty depressing to think that Da hasn't even noticed. It's even more depressing to think that he has but he doesn't like the atmosphere any more than I do.

I'm attaching my Liverpool jersey to the line with a plastic peg and I'm saying, 'Not too bad. How's it going with you, Derek?'

Our yard is a little concrete-floored oblong, walled-in by a four-foot-high perimeter of grey unpainted blocks. The concrete floor is breaking up and weeds are unfurling through it in brilliant green.

Derek coughs into one yellow hand and in that cough you can hear the wet slapping of his decaying lungs.

He goes to say something, coughs again and hawks up a wad of phlegm that he spits into a tissue.

I go, 'Are you alright, Derek?'

He nods and goes, 'I'm fine. It's quare hard to kill a bad thing.'

I laugh and go to hang up one of Da's T-shirts when Derek stops me in my tracks.

Just like that he goes, 'You'd want to watch that Guard Devlin.'

I'm blinking at him now and I don't know what to say.

Derek laughs and the laugh turns into a spluttering rasp and he wheezes, 'Sorry. Sorry. I was talking to your Da and he said you'd gotten into a bit of trouble. He mentioned that guard.'

I'm nodding silently still holding the sopping T-shirt and Derek is going, 'Well, I'd be quare careful of him. He's not exactly a straight arrow.'

I'm frowning now and I'm going, 'How do you mean?'

Derek looks around him like he's in a fucking pantomime and he whispers with the rasp of each of his sixty Sweet Afton a day fraying his voice. He leans over the wall and he goes, 'Remember the brothel that they shut down a few months ago? The one in that house up by Cluain Árd?'

I'm stepping closer to him now and my mind is full of curiosity. Full of the Hardy Boys and Nancy Drew.

I'm now part of Derek's little cloak and dagger show and I say, 'Go on.'

Derek goes, 'Well, they say that Devlin was mixed up in it somehow and that it was all swept under the carpet.'

Still frowning, I'm going, 'Who says, Derek?'

And like he's a fucking a pirate or something, Derek says, '*Iiiii* says.'

He says, 'A few months ago I was caught short coming home from Mackey's and I went for a piss down by the gasworks beside the Slaney. The squad car rolled up with Devlin and this other young fella in it.'

He shakes his head and goes, 'It's quare bad when you can't even go for a piss without the guards sticking their snouts in.'

I don't say anything to this.

Derek is still talking. He's saying, 'Devlin and the young guard got out of the car and Devlin said to me, "For fuck's sake. You're worse than a dog."

'Of course, I'm fluthered out of me skull and like an eejit I threw the brothel thing back into his big fat fucking face.'

Then Derek laughs again and in it you can hear the clattering of coffin lids. He goes, 'He has some size fuckin head doesn't he? Big fuckin farmer's son I bet.'

In my mind, I can see Guard Devlin's muscled ham of a head. Like a Great White's. I can see the teeth in his smile. His barbed-wire grin.

Derek goes, 'The big bollix nearly took my fuckin head off with a box. And do you know what he said to me when I'm lying on the ground? Do you what he said? Cos I can remember every single fuckin word.'

I'm shaking my head and Derek is saying, 'He leaned down over me and he spat, he fuckin *spat*, right in my face and he said to me, "There's a lot of deep holes in this river. They'll only look for you where I tell them to look for you."'

Now Derek spits himself and goes, 'Cunt.'

I'm swallowing something that feels like chalk dust in my throat and I go, 'What happened then?'

Derek snorts and says, 'The two of them put the boot in a few times and then fucked off. The next day, I went up to the barracks to complain but they laughed me out of the fuckin place.'

Derek eyes me with shrewd little button eyes and he goes, 'I'd watch myself with that one. Don't cross him. He's bad news.'

I'm standing there as Derek is saying this and I'm hoping that it's the dripping T-shirt that's making my pants wet.

It takes about a week for Seán to decide to stop his meds.

He has long chats with Mr Cowper and he's in the Guidance Office more than he's in class. On the corridors people still woof and bark and pretend to scratch behind their ears. I'm getting this every bit as much as Seán and I'm trying to cope with it but it isn't easy. Every time my phone goes off my stomach knots because it might be one of the lads texting me a picture of a dead dog. I haven't gone on Facebook in ages because it's just one solid mess of abuse and insults.

Most of the lads think they're only slagging but day after day of this is starting to wear me down.

Seán doesn't tell anyone that he's stopped taking the tablets but it's pretty obvious. His face isn't as sad anymore and there's colour back in his voice. He doesn't sound like a robot anymore. He actually seems happier but every now and then when the lads *woof* at us I can see something crawl beneath his skin. Seán doesn't want to do bad things but I don't think he can help himself. Every day he's fighting a battle that he can't win because what he's fighting is himself.

Just like before I don't know what it's costing Seán to keep himself under control but the pressure will tell in the end. He'll snap just like he did with the dead dogs.

We only have the time between now and then to do something about Dr Thorpe. Then Seán can go back to his meds. He can go back to wherever it is they send him, a world wrapped in wet wool.

I feel like I'm using him. I feel like he's my crutch in all this.

The thing is, I have no idea what to do.

My Da is happy enough now that he thinks Seán is drugged to the eyeballs and he's encouraging me to spend more time with him. He says this is because the summer holidays are coming up and Seán needs help with his English but I know it's really because something has changed between us. A glass wall has come down and me and my Da aren't the way we used to be. I haven't seen him laugh in weeks.

Me and Seán are sitting in his bedroom in his house out by the Still. His bedroom is pretty big, like my one used to be when I lived out here with Mam and Da. He has a single bed against one wall and his laptop sits on a desk in the corner. Normally when you visit your mates their rooms are covered in posters. Premiership teams and action shots of Suarez or Giggs or Lampard. Posters of musicians and singers and glossy shots of Cheryl Cole with just the right amount of cleavage showing. People pretend that their parents don't really notice this but we all know that they do, they just don't mention it.

Not Seán's room, though.

Seán's room is like a cell. There aren't any posters on the walls and there aren't any pictures of family or friends. Each wall is a blank arctic yawn of white paint. Here and there you can see dim smudges of ancient Bl-Tack where something used to hang. They are like the marks left on people's forehead after mass on Ash Wednesday. What happened is a few years ago Seán's Da got a bit freaked out by the fact that Seán spent so much of his time in a featureless box. Seán's Da thought his son needed more stimulation than to just be walled in by white. When Seán was out, his Da went and stuck maybe half a dozen posters to the walls. When Seán came back he started to moan until his Da took them all back down again.

Seán tells me after this that he can't sleep with posters on his walls. He thinks the people in them are looking at him and that they move around when he closes his eyes. When he tells me this I tell him not to be so fucking stupid but when I'm going to sleep that night I keep thinking about the eyes of all the two-dimensional footballers staring at me.

We're sitting in Seán's room and there's no posters, no books, no magazines. Nothing except me and Seán and the little tub of tablets that he's shaking in his fist.

He's going, 'I feel okay. I don't feel like I'm going to do anything bad.'

I'm nodding at him and I'm saying, 'Good. So what are we going to do about Dr Thorpe?'

Seán shrugs and he goes, 'I don't want to get into any more trouble.'

I can see the set to his shoulders, the stubborness underneath. This has been missing for the past while. Any sense of vitality was leached out of him. Seán might be an oddball but at least he's alive again.

I'm looking at him and I'm going, 'We won't get in trouble. We just need to find some way to prove we saw Dr Thorpe . . .'

And now I'm stopping. I can't bring myself to actually say the words and Seán is looking at me all confused and so I just say, '. . . doing what he did.'

I look at the floor between my runners and when I look up again Seán is not looking at me. He's looking off over my left shoulder and his eyes have this thousand-yard stare to them. It's like he's seeing something that nobody else can. His face has an expression that falls somewhere between confusion and surprise.

There's this theory about the universal nature of the spirit. I saw it somewhere on the Discovery Channel or something. You take four ordinary people from four different cultures. An American, an Englishman, an Indian and a Japanese person. Now to these four people you give an identical drug. Ethics are circumvented here by the fact that they're all volunteers. The fact that the drug induces vomiting, diarrhoea, fever and hallucinations is, however, impossible to get around. Poor bastards. But this is all in the cause of scientific enquiry so that's okay too.

In fact it's the vomiting, diarrhoea, fever and hallucinations that makes it all worthwhile. It's the point.

The drug comes from some root or plant or sap or something only found in the Amazon. In fact it's only found in a particular part of the Amazon. You know all those eco-warriors bleating on about how hectares of potential cancer cures are being torched or turned into sawdust every day? Well hectares of interesting shit like this are going up in smoke too. In fact, since I don't have cancer, interesting shit holds a lot more relevance for me.

This shit is interesting due to the effect it has on the four volunteers. The schmucks.

You see the vomiting, diarrhoea, fever and hallucinations have the strange quality of being the exact same for them all. Especially the hallucinations.

The drug from the root or plant or sap has been taken forever by the traditional, indigenous shamans of a tribe who still retain an almost placental connection with the earth which . . . whatever. Basically the local priests take this stuff to get themselves high. They vomit, they shit, they shake and finally they see things. What they see is this. First they're in a field of maize. Maize so high it's like a solid wall of green and gold. Then a jaguar, yeah a jaguar, comes and takes their hands in its mouth and leads them off. Anthropologists and sociologists explain this by saying that jaguars and maize are part of the culture and aren't just brought about by the drug's effects. They see maize and jaguars because that's what they expect to see.

This is where the experiment comes in.

If you give this drug to four people from four other places, other social spheres, other worlds, and don't tell them what to expect except shits and spits and shakes and some pretty colours, will they see jaguars too? Place your bets ladies and gentlemen, the ball is rolling.

And guess what? They all saw a field of maize and they all saw the jaguar.

This can be explained by either some wacky property of the drug which short-circuits the connection between our hind-brain and consciousness and shoves an image of some primordial big cat into our thoughts. Or else some wacky property of the drug kicks open the Doors and leads us to a place where jaguars act as guides. They're both pretty fucked up in my opinion.

The professor whose job it was to rationalise this madness to the viewing public started to laugh halfway through. I remember this. I remember his olive cardigan and his reasonable, oh-so-serious face. I remember the twitch at the corner of his mouth just before he started to laugh. I remember how he tried to hide the mania in that laugh. It was like he'd had a hole punched in his world and couldn't help but look into it.

This is how Seán looks now.

It's like he's looking into a different world.

And then he's going, 'We could spy on him.'

I'm blinking at him because he hasn't said anything constructive in so long. He definitely wouldn't be saying this stuff if he was still on his meds.

He's saying, 'He must have put the body somewhere. It wasn't there when we went in. I didn't like his house. It smells weird. I don't like Dr Thorpe anymore.'

I'm smiling at Seán and now I'm really happy he's off his meds. In spite of everything, I'm smiling.

I'm going, 'I don't like him either.'

Seán is nodding and smiling back at me and he goes, 'He plays golf. I seen him loads of times. He always has his clubs in his car. He has lots of golf stuff in his house.'

And suddenly I'm thinking about the plaque on his desk. *Strawberry Fair Golf Classic Winner 2009 2010 2011.*

I'm looking at Seán and my grin is so wide that it's hurting my jaws.

'Seán,' I go, 'you're a genius.'

Seán used to be like this all the time. In spite of his weirdness. In spite of the way he does *things* to things. He always used to have a current running through him. Something more than just a spark.

This all started to change around the time that his Mam left. Something soured in him.

No, that's wrong.

What that implies is that there's some causal relationship between Seán's Mam leaving and his internal wiring starting to short out in a bad way. It's like there's a row of dominos with his Mam's face on the first one and a picture of dead dogs on the last. This just isn't true.

His Mam leaving has fuck all to do with his problems. His Da hitting him might though.

This one time just after his Mam walks out, Seán is playing with me and the lads in Alex DeCourcey's house. Alex DeCourcey's little sister has a bunch of rabbits and guinea pigs that live in this little hutch made out of timber and chicken wire. The little sister doesn't really give a fuck about her box of rodents but God help you if you go near them. She doesn't even know how many she has. She doesn't even feed them.

We are paying absolutely no attention to the rabbits and guinea pigs because Alex DeCourcey has managed to get his hands on his big brother's collection of *Nuts* magazines. The day is cold, I remember this, cold and windy because whenever you let go of the pages the wind whips them closed.

Me and the lads are hiding behind the coal shed in Alex DeCourcey's back yard and we are all amazed by pictures of half-naked, air-brushed models. All of us are trying to stop the breeze fluttering shut the pages. All of us except Seán.

Seán is standing over at the rabbit hutch and he's smiling away to himself because Alex DeCourcey's Mam has given him lettuce leaves to feed to the rabbits. Seán couldn't care less about anything in *Nuts* magazine.

Things start to go wrong when Seán goes to put his hand inside the rabbit hutch. He doesn't want to open the door because it's locked and, to Seán's mind, if there's a lock on something it's there for a reason. However, he doesn't see anything wrong with trying to shove his hand into a slight gap between the chicken wire and the timber frame.

When me and Alex DeCourcey and the rest of the lads come out from behind the coal shed with our faces red and our heads full of fake boobs and shiny lipstick the first thing we see is Seán lying on his belly with one arm shoved into the rabbit hutch. His arm is all the way in, right up to the elbow and all the rabbits and guinea pigs are gathered in this mound of fur and twitching whiskers at the far end of the hutch. Seán's ass is sticking in the air and he's squirming like an eel because he's after getting his arm stuck in the chicken wire. From across the yard you can hear him moaning as if he's about to cry.

Me and the lads go and stand over him and Seán goes, 'My arm is stuck. I didn't mean to.'

To help him out, me and Alex DeCourcey grab an ankle each and we heft him backwards. He sticks for a second and then comes loose so suddenly that me and Alex nearly end up falling on our arses. He comes loose so suddenly that the rabbit hutch rattles on its moorings and the rabbits and guinea pigs all make this weird piping noise.

Everyone laughs and Seán sits there smiling in inane gratitude and then we all go and play football. An hour later, Seán runs away with the ball and we all go home.

So much, so ordinary.

The thing that nobody notices is that, when we pull Seán free, his big arm is after widening the gap between the chicken wire and timber frame. His big arm is after widening it just enough so that one particularly determined guinea pig can fit through and make a dash for freedom. Can guinea pigs dash? Anyway, said guinea pig makes it as far as the road and then a passing car turns it into red paste. The driver doesn't even stop.

This happens at night and Alex DeCourcey's little sister

discovers what's left of her guinea pig the next morning. She discovers what's left of her guinea pig and she will just not stop crying.

This is where things get bad for Seán.

There's a big parental enquiry about who fucked up the rabbit hutch and Alex DeCourcey squeals and blames Seán. This is utter crap because it was probably me and Alex who ruined it by dragging Seán out of it by the ankles. We dragged him because we thought it would be a laugh. Nobody's laughing now, especially not Alex's little sister.

Alex's Mam calls around to Seán's Da and she gives him both barrels. All of us except Seán are out in the road pretending to be playing football. Seán's Da stands there saying nothing. He stands there in an Ireland football jersey from about 1994 and he just lets her words sleet over him. He hasn't got that waxy look off him yet. His skin doesn't look like yellow lard but it's starting to. Even from the road you can tell he's drunk as a maggot and his eyes are all whorled about with black wrinkles.

Alex's Mam goes, 'What are you going to do about it?'

And Seán's Da says, 'Do? I'll do plenty.'

And then he's roaring, 'Seán! Seán! Get your arse down here!'

Seán doesn't get his arse down there. In fact nobody knows where Seán is. We all search up and down the road for him. Even his Da.

When we find him it is at the back of Alex DeCoursey's house and he has a guinea pig in his arms. Alex's Mam goes crazy at this and Seán's Da grabs him by the collar and hauls him home. Alex's little sister grabs the guinea pig and puts it in the hutch with the others.

The thing about this is that everyone goes hysterical without asking Seán anything. Everyone is so wound up that their nerves are razor wire beneath their skin and they can't think straight. Nobody talks to Seán and nobody listens when he tries to explain.

The next day me and Seán are sitting on his wall and he won't tell me what happened to his lips, what happened to his eye. He just stares at the ground and in a voice that's all slurred and slushy because of his busted mouth, he tells me why he was holding the guinea pig.

It turns out that Seán got up real early that morning and went to look at the guinea pigs and rabbits again. He couldn't sleep for thinking about them. It turns out that Seán was the first person on the road that morning, the very first person, to realise what happened to Alex's sister's guinea pig.

Seán isn't stupid.

It also turns out that Seán had about twenty quid saved up for the new FIFA due out in a month or so.

Seán, being Seán, feels terrible about what happened. He feels like he's to blame and that he's going to get into trouble. So, feeling like this he goes back and gets his twenty quid and, still feeling like this, he walks into town and he buys Alex's sister a new guinea pig.

When Alex's Mam goes all psycho on him he was just trying to replace the dead one. The one he blamed himself for getting killed.

And nobody listens to him and nobody asks him any questions and his Da just hammers the tar out of him.

Even back then, that morning sitting on the wall, I can see the change that Seán's undergone. He's still Seán but something's hardened in him. There's an edge to his smile that I don't like. An awful glee. His grin is like a sickle ever since.

There's three weeks to go till the summer holidays. When they kick in, me and Seán are going to do something about Dr Thorpe.

We have this all worked out.

The Friday after school ends is the start of the Strawberry Fair. Dr Thorpe with his big car and hair is going to head off playing golf all day. He does this every year. His face is always plastered all over next week's *Echo* accepting a trophy from the Club Captain. Every year this happens. Regular as breathing. I remember Dr Thorpe calling out to our house when Mam was sick and Da hooting laughing with him about playing off eleven when he should be playing off four or five.

I fucking *hate* golf.

We, me and Seán, are going to wait until the coast is clear and then we're going to do our best to see if we can find anything at his house or in his garden. Anything at all.

The three weeks until the holidays crawl along like something gutted and dying a slow death. Every day, every single day, me and Seán get caught in a blizzard of woofs and yelps and howls.

For the summer exams our Irish teacher includes a comprehension on a lost dog. Maybe I'm being paranoid but I'm pretty sure he's taking the piss.

School for Seán isn't really working without his meds. There's a static charge building in him with every minute he spends in the place and it's going to have to be earthed somewhere. He spends most of the day with Mr Cowper and he spends his lunchtimes sitting on a windowsill with his face in his hands. I feel really, really guilty about this.

Nobody wants to talk to us. Nobody texts and nobody rings and it's like we're cut off from everybody else. Pariahs.

Football in the yard is a joke. I'm the school's Under-18 keeper and nobody picks me for a kick around anymore. I can't wait for this year to end.

And Judas is gibbering away all the time, *This is all Seán's fault. I don't know why the fuck people think you're a weirdo too. He cut open that dog, for fuck's sake. Not you.*

But I ignore him and he fades into the background and I concentrate on proving what we know about Dr Thorpe. I can't do this without Seán. I hate to admit it but I'm nowhere near strong enough.

I make a complete hames of my summer exams. I make a complete hames of everything except English. The report won't be posted out until July but I know that I've failed at least four subjects out of seven. It's not that I'm stupid or lazy but I can't concentrate on anything other than the plan for the first day of the Strawberry Fair. When I should be studying Maths, I start making rough sketches of Dr Thorpe's property. When it's time for a change, instead of Geography I'm labelling the sketches in BLOCK CAPITALS. Here's the house and here's the driveway.

See also the electric gates.

See also the eight-foot wall.

See also the rose beds.

Everything nice and precise.

I text Seán every few minutes and he replies every single time. I check my phone at one stage and my inbox has 129 messages. All except one is from Seán. The exception is the one from my Da telling me to turn down the speakers for my iPod and go to sleep.

We finish school and the following Friday is the start of the Strawberry Fair. That Thursday night I can't sleep. I keep twisting in the bed and my stomach is a twitching swamp of nausea. I'm not sure if I can go through with this. A good few times I pick up my phone and start to text Seán to tell him to forget about this whole thing. And every time I see Dr Thorpe's slow, born-to-be-a-winner smile and I hear his fist connecting with cartilage.

The dead meat smack of it.

Every time I remember this I delete the words I've written on my phone and I lie there with my brain a lump of sweating tar in my skull. I'm so tired it feels like my eyeballs are filmed with dust. Every blink feels like sandpaper. I lie like this for I don't know how long but when the bedroom starts to brighten, I know I have to get up.

It is six o'clock and all is not fucking well.

I get up, dress myself, and really quietly I sneak out the front door. All the time my heart is thud-tha-thudding under my ribs. If my Da wakes up and starts asking questions I don't know what I'll say.

The door clicks shut behind me and I freeze on the doorstep. I'm waiting for my Da to lean out his bedroom window and call me back. Nothing happens though and after a minute I head across the bridge and up past the Castle. The Market Square is empty apart from a skinny black mongrel that limps away from me on three good legs. The entire place is covered in purple and gold and red and white bunting. There's a big trailer after being hauled into the Square and there are speakers set up and ready to be plugged in. In front of the trailer white lawn furniture is stacked waiting for the pensioners and the children and the spilled ice cream.

Up past the Cathedral Seán is waiting for me outside Kelly's shop and in spite of my nerves I'm grinning at him.

Seán blinks at me and he goes, 'This is too early.'

He's wrong on this one. We have to be ready to hop over Dr Thorpe's wall as soon as we get the chance. I looked in the *Echo* for the tee-off times for the Golf Classic and the earliest two-ball is scheduled for half-past seven. If Dr Thorpe is playing first we might miss our chance to poke around his garden.

I'm looking at Seán and I'm shaking my head and I'm going, 'It's not too early. We're bang on time.'

And then I'm going, 'Did you bring them?'

Seán reaches a big paw into his hoodie pocket and pulls out a half pound of sausages. These are for Dr Thorpe's dog in case she gets all brave in herself all of a sudden.

Seán holds the bundle of sausages in the bundle of his own sausage fingers and he looks down at them and he starts to frown.

Before he has the chance to say anything I'm going, 'We don't have time for breakfast. There's nowhere open anyway. Later on. Afterwards.'

Seán tuts like he's a child and he tucks the sausages back into his pocket.

We, me and Seán, walk down Nunnery Road but instead of going straight to Dr Thorpe's we climb up the hill to the grotto and we sit on the benches and we watch Dr Thorpe's gate. Because of the Strawberry Fair the barricades are already up to stop people driving into the centre of town and the road below us is deserted. This is traditional because one time this really pissed fifty-year-old woman in a Land Rover tried to drive down into the Square. The guards pretty much hauled her out by the hair. Nothing is moving and my skin is bubbling up with goosebumps. It's like every inch of me is covered in little nettle stings. My adrenaline is at such a pitch that my stomach is in constant spasm. If I did have time for breakfast I'd be spewing it all over the grotto's nice paving slabs right about now.

Seán is sitting beside me and every now and then he throws a look towards the statue of Our Lady standing in her little nook. She is staring off at a spot in the sky and her hands are steepled under her chin. Her paint is starting to flake away after all these

years and her eyes are blank and white and blind as spiders'
eggs.

Seán throws the statue another look and he goes, 'Did she
really move?'

Without taking my eyes off Dr Thorpe's front gate I say, 'No.
She never moved.'

And Seán goes, 'Da says that during the eighties she moved
and you could pray to her for stuff.'

Still not taking my eyes off Dr Thorpe's front gate I say, 'Well,
go ahead and pray then.'

Seán sits there for a minute and then he puts his hands together and he squeezes his eyes shut and just like that he goes, 'Dear
Mary. Help us.'

And just like that Dr Thorpe's big black iron gates give a little
shudder and start to open up with a noise like scrap being
crushed. A few seconds later Dr Thorpe's oil-sleek 407 slides out
onto the road, turns left because Nunnery Road is closed to traffic, cruises up to the roundabout at the top of Bohreen Hill,
swings right and disappears.

I watch it go and beside me Seán's blessing himself and he
says, 'Dear Mary. Thank you.'

Me and Seán walk down to the road and we follow Dr
Thorpe's eight-foot concrete wall around to the side of his property. There's no way we can get over it the way we did in the dark
so we have to plough our way through all the bracken and all the
briars that fill this little scrap of wasteland behind Dr Thorpe's
garden. When we get round the back we are in a little alley

swarfed with briar and hedged in by blackthorns, and the back wall of Dr Thorpe's garden rears up on our left. All along the base of the wall there's a drift of decaying grass cuttings. Month after month, year after year Dr Thorpe must cut his grass and dump it over the wall. The stuff is slumped all together in lumpen strata, the top ones green and smelling like summer, the bottom ones putrefying into brown slush.

We stand here breathing in the smells of the slowly decaying grass and Seán sticks his thumb in his mouth because he's hooked it on a briar. Around his thumb his voice comes all distorted. It goes, 'What do we do now?'

I'm looking at the wall and I'm accutely aware that I don't know how much time we have.

I look at Seán and I look at the wall and I go, 'If I boost you up could you lift me?'

Seán nods once. This time he's not afraid he'll drop me.

Seán weighs a tonne and from the platform of my cupped hands he half hops, half scrabbles to the top of the wall. He lies on his belly and he reaches down his hand and he grins at me. There are blades in that grin and I'm wondering if Seán is about to crack again.

Then I think of Dr Thorpe and then, trying not to think of anything else, I grab Seán's hand and I sort of scramble up the wall.

I'm out of breath and the two of us sit there for a minute looking down on Dr Thorpe's garden.

Dr Thorpe's garden is about a half acre of soft green lawn. In the sunlight you can see that he's cut the lawn all fancy so that it looks like there are areas of lighter and darker grass all in the shape of diamonds. The whole middle of the lawn is taken up by a big spiral bed of roses. The bare earth of the flowerbeds is covered with more quilts of decaying grass. Dr Thorpe's house sits at the far end of this half acre of grass and roses, and to the left there's a concrete straggle of sheds with galvanised roofs. One of the sheds is open and hanging on a nail on the door jamb is a dog collar and a choke chain.

We, me and Seán, sit there for a minute taking this all in and Seán goes, 'Dr Thorpe has a really nice garden. Maybe we shouldn't jump down. I don't want to get in trouble.'

I'm looking at him and I'm saying, 'I can't do this on my own, Seán. I have to find out what happened to that girl. Everyone thinks we're freaks. If we can show them that we saw what we saw then maybe people will change their minds.'

Seán looks from me to the lawn and back again and he goes, 'People think I'm a freak all the time.'

Then he stops and lifts up his big hands and he clenches and opens them, clenches and opens them. He looks at them like it's the first time he's ever noticed them and he says, 'I don't like being a freak.'

And I'm saying, 'Neither do I.'

Without another word the two of us are climbing down into Dr Thorpe's garden. As soon as the soles of my runners touch Dr Thorpe's mint-green lawn my heart starts to paradiddle against my ribs. I can feel every hot gush of its workings.

As soon as the soles of my runners touch Dr Thorpe's mint-green lawn his German Pointer comes trotting out of her shed.

The dog is this lovely soft grey colour all splotched with daubs of chocolate. Her head is a chocolate wedge and two intelligent gold eyes take in me and Seán standing stock-still against the wall. The dog stops and the hackles raise on the back of her neck and she makes this weird whuffling noise halfway between a bark and a growl. She takes two quick steps forward and this time she lets out this little yipping bark like she doesn't quite mean it yet but she's getting there.

Then Seán is moving past me so that he stands between me and the dog and he goes, 'Here, girl. You're a good dog, aren't you? Here, girl.'

He has the half pound of sausages in his hand. The German Pointer looks like she's going to turn around and run the hell away but then her wet pad of a nose lifts and she takes a step towards Seán.

Seán's going, 'Good girl. Good girl.'

There's a softness in his voice that I've never heard before and he's staring at the dog like he's amazed by her.

The dog takes another few steps forward and now Seán is giving her the sausages. The dog sniffs at them and then she starts wolfing them down with Seán standing over her, his big hand stroking her back and smoothing the place where her hackles had all bristled up.

I let him stroke her for a minute and then I go, 'Seán! We have to get moving. If Dr Thorpe comes back we're fucked.'

Seán doesn't move. He just stands there smiling and petting the dog.

I'm looking at the house and the hairs on the back of my neck are starting to stand up and I'm going, 'Seán! For fuck's sake. We may hurry up. If Dr Thorpe catches us here he'll kill us too.

This seems to trigger something in Seán because he slowly turns around and there's this strange dopey expression on his face like he's been anaesthetized or something.

There's this poem we're doing in school and one of the lines goes, *like a patient etherized upon a table*. Seán is upright but this is exactly him. Etherized.

Slowly he says, 'Yeah. We may. She's real soft. Her hair is real soft.'

The dog follows me and Seán as we walk around the garden looking for anywhere that could be used to hide a body. Looking for any evidence of anything at all. The garden is wide open and apart from the sheds there's absolutely nowhere that anyone could hide anything. We look under a wheelbarrow that's upside-down against the wall of one shed. Its flat tyre is a fat slug of rubber, heavy on its axle.

The sheds aren't locked so we open them and look in. They're all ridiculously neat inside with tools hanging on racks and garden furniture all stacked like the furniture for the Strawberry Fair. Even the dog shed is pristine. There's a sort of loft under the roof in the dog shed and we even climb into that but there's nothing up there except forty-litre bags of grass seed and Presto dog food.

We even go right up to the house and look through the kitchen windows. Seán makes the mistake of pressing his face against a window pane and the fats in his sweat leave a halloween mask of his features on the glass. I'm cursing at him because I'm frustrated and feeling stupid and he starts to moan because I'm giving out to him and all the while Dr Thorpe's German Pointer follows us around with her bright eyes and her little spud of a tail wagging like crazy.

Around the garden there is nothing. There is absolutely nothing to suggest that Dr Thorpe murdered anyone. The place looks like it's cut and pasted straight out of *Gardener's Weekly*. There's not one blade of grass out of place. Not one fork or spade has even the smallest clot of soil or dirt clinging to it. Everything is elegant and meticulous and I feel like an idiot.

For the first time since all this started, Seán's looking at me like he doesn't believe me.

His mouth opens and he goes, 'Are you sure he hid her here?'

I'm frowning at him and I go, 'No, I'm not fucking sure. I'm not sure that she's even within a hundred miles of here. I just thought we might find something. Anything.'

Seán's face scrunches up and he goes to say something but then stops.

I'm looking at him and I'm saying, 'Go on. Out with it.'

And Seán looks at me and he goes, 'Are you sure you saw what you saw?'

Before I can answer there's that scrap crushing noise again from beyond the house and the German Pointer pricks up her ears and lets out this little excited whine. Seán and me look at each other for a moment with our foreheads all creased and then the sound of tyres on gravel makes both our mouths drop open like our jaws are dislocated.

There's a sudden panic in me that's so intense it's like it's going to swallow the world. The edges of my vision are all blotted with shadow and I think I'm actually going to faint. I don't know how long we, me and Seán, stand like this staring at each other but at the sound of a car door opening the German Pointer runs around to the front of the house.

From over the keel of the roof we can hear Dr Thorpe's voice, not shouting but getting there. Into his phone or something he's going, 'I'm not playing without my rescue wood. It'll take two minutes, Darragh. Two fucking minutes.'

And in his voice there's just the merest suggestion of the violence squirming in him.

And then another voice carries in the summer air all thick and heavy as a midlands bog, 'A rescue wood? If I find *it* still in that shed you'll need more than a fucking rescue wood.'

Then Seán's shaking himself like he's just waking up and he's going, 'We have to leave. I don't want to get in trouble.'

And automatically I'm answering him. I'm saying, 'You won't get into trouble.' But I don't know if this is the truth or not. I'm terrified.

I'm looking at the back wall of Dr Thorpe's garden. It is suddenly light years away. There's absolutely no chance of me and Seán getting over it before Dr Thorpe sees us. If he comes straight into the kitchen we won't even get as far as the rose beds.

Then Seán goes, 'We can hide in the dog shed.'

I'm blinking and it's like the machinery of my brain is all seized up and rusted solid.

Seán's looking afraid too and he's staring at me and he's going, 'We can hide up in the roof. Behind the dog food.'

I'm nodding because I can't say anything. Every drop of moisture has evaporated from my throat. I can feel my tongue stick to the roof of my mouth like something charred in a stove. Without much conscious thought I'm running beside Seán. Running through the sunlight and the smells of roses. Running until we reach the dog shed.

No shout pursues us or halts us in our tracks. No noise comes from the doctor's house.

The dog shed is an oven in the lifting sun and from the shadowed corners and the bowl of dog food there's the sickbed buzzing of flies. We climb up into the little loft and burrow in amongst the bags of dog food and grass seed. We lie there baking under the galvanise and we try to stop our breathing from sounding too loud. I'm sure if you stood at the open door you'd be able to hear the woolly hammering of my heart. Of my panic.

Seán's trying to stop himself moaning but every now and then this noise comes lowing soft from between his clenched teeth.

When I hear voices, I freeze.

Beside me I can feel the cords of Seán's too-big muscles tighten and then he goes still as well. He lies there, hard and motionless as a concrete slab.

Outside in the garden I can hear Dr Thorpe going, 'Good girl. Look at the fat belly on you. Come on and we'll fill up your water. Good girl.'

And then another voice trails in on the slick of sunlight coming through the door. It goes, 'How old is she now? Are you thinking of breeding her?'

I recognise that voice. The dragged-out wide vowels. The funny Rs.

Guard Devlin.

Then between the bags of grass seed and dog food I can see two shadows at the door. Then between the bags of grass seed and dog food I can see the two men.

Guard Devlin is in full uniform. His hat is crammed down on his head so that from where I'm lying I can't see his eyes. Over his pale blue shirt his stab vest is a wall of navy panelling. Beside him, Dr Thorpe is wearing cream slacks and a red polo shirt and he reaches down to pick up his dog's half-empty water bowl, its contents gone stagnant in the heat.

His hair glimmers in the sunshine as he's straightening up and saying, 'I might breed her alright. I don't do much hunting anymore.'

And the guard's going, 'No? No, I suppose you don't. Doing a lot of gardening these days, I see. Did you ever see *Tales of the Unexpected*? Rose bushes. Everything was all the time buried under rose bushes.'

It's Dr Thorpe's reaction that makes me almost gasp out loud.

He grabs the guard by the front of his stab-proof vest and

drags him all the way into the dog shed. His face is all twisted up and he looks like he's goig to explode. His face is the colour of wet brick dust and there's a purple worm of vein scrawled all the way down from one temple to underneath his left eye.

He has the guard by the front of his vest and he's spraying words into his face. He's going, 'For fuck's sake, Ted. That's not a fucking laughing matter. Do you know what it's like to be accused of something so horrible? Jesus Christ.'

The guard has his hands up with the palms out and he's going, 'Easy, Syl. Take it easy. I didn't mean to upset you.'

Dr Thorpe lets him go and looks down at the clean cement floor. He shakes his head and goes, 'I'm sorry, Ted. I've been under a lot of stress lately. This has been very hard.'

Guard Devlin folds his arms and goes, 'Look. It's all taken care of. I couldn't care less even if she was pushing up roses.'

And there it is.

Beside me I can feel Seán spasm and the plastic bags of seed and grain crackle softly.

Pushing up roses.

Guard Devlin and Dr Thorpe don't notice though and Dr Thorpe's going, 'I don't know how you can be so cavalier about all this.'

The guard is leaning against the door jamb now and his alien voice is coming out from under the brim of his cap. He's saying, 'I'm not being cavalier at all. I can guarantee you that. But, Syl, if you want me to do anything else for you, you'll have to wait a while.'

Dr Thorpe is shaking his head now and he's going, 'We'll see. We'll see.'

Then he looks down to where he's dropped the dog's bowl. Stagnant water has splashed all over the cement floor and made dark lozenges all over the front of his slacks.

He says, 'Fuck.'

Then he picks up the bowl, goes to a tap by the shed door and fill the bowl again. He puts it on the ground and drags his damp fingers through his hairspray-cured quiff. He sighs when he does this and the guard goes, 'Go and play your golf. Forget about this.'

Then the two men turn and leave the dog shed. The last thing I hear before they get too far away is Guard Devlin going, 'I'll say this though, Syl. You need to get a grip on that temper of yours.'

We, me and Seán, stay hiding behind the bags of seed and dog food for another fifteen minutes. We stay there so long that my shirt feels like it's been drenched in warm water and sweat is dripping from my eyebrows. We stay there for fifteen minutes not saying a anything. And for fifteen minutes the words *pushing up roses* are cycling through my brain. Round and round and round.

Eventually Dr Thorpe's German Pointer pads into the shed and sits on the warm cement floor looking up at us. She whimpers way down in the back of her throat.

Seán goes, 'What do we do now? Are we in trouble?'

And I go, 'No. We're not in trouble. We're fucking right. We've been right all along. I did see something. I knew it.'

The dead meat smack of it.

And Seán turns his big head and he says, 'So are we going home?'

He says, 'Are we ringing the Guards?'

He says, 'I don't like this place.'

And looking at his soft sweating face I know he's going to have a hard time understanding all this.

I go, 'We can't ring the Guards because they seem to be in on this. If we ring them we might end up pushing up roses too.'

Seán's frowning and his cheeks are oceans of perspiration. He's frowning and he says, 'What does *pushing up roses* mean?'

He's looking at me like he hasn't heard the conversation between Dr Thorpe and Guard Devlin. He's looking at me with a strange searching look on his face. His eyes slither over my features like leeches.

He's looking at me like this and then he's going, 'Tell me.'

And with my heart still slam-dancing against my ribs I say, 'I can't tell you.

'I can't tell you,' I say again. 'But I can show you.'

The spades in Dr Thorpe's sheds are all ridiculously well maintained. The handles are worn and sweat-lacquered to a matt sheen and the blades are all shiny and oiled and free from rust and muck. You could perform surgery with them. Or an autopsy.

I grab one and Seán grabs another and the two of us go over to the big spiral rose bed. Dr Thorpe's German Pointer tags along after Seán. We get to the rose bed and we start to scoop away the mulch and dead grass. At the beginning Seán has no idea why he's doing this but the longer we keep at it the more the realisation dawns on him.

He stops and goes, 'What if we find her?'

I look at him and the heat of my efforts is dribbling sweat into my eyes and scalding them.

He stops and goes, 'Maybe we should ring your Da or someone.'

I look at him in disgust and go, 'Because that did a whole lot of good the last time?'

I've cleared a big swathe of mulch and dead grass and it's lying scattered all over the lawn next to the rose bed. When Dr Thorpe comes back it'll be obvious what's after happening and if we're still here I'm pretty sure we're dead. Now I'm standing on the raw soil of the rose bed. Wexford soil, dark as molasses, and my spade bites into it and throws it out and away.

And then Dr Thorpe's German Pointer comes up beside me and starts scratching right beside where I'm digging.

I'm looking at the dog and I realise that Seán has stopped digging and he's watching too. The dog's two front paws are churning the soil and she's yipping to herself, soft but frantic.

And now I'm going, 'Seán, could you come here and hold the dog, please?'

I'm calm. Calm as a graveyard.

Seán's hand on the dog's neck stops her digging and Seán half-lifts half-drags the dog away. When the dog is out of the way I start ramming the spade into the grooves her paws have carved.

I dig for ten minutes and then I dig for ten minutes more with the fats in my body melting in the heat and drooling out of my pores.

I'm thinking, what if I find something?

When I start to retch I'm glad I haven't eaten anything.

The noises I'm making frighten the dog and she ducks behind Seán's legs. I stand there doubled over and every muscle in my torso is aching because I'm dry-heaving so hard. My throat is burning because my stomach is trying to eject bile and acid out through my mouth.

Seán just stands there and looks at me like I'm not me anymore. Already there's flies starting to land in the crater at my feet. From out of it I think I can get the stink of something rotting. It smells like that gutted house. Like dead dogs.

The crater is about two feet down under this lovely cottage rose. I can't see it yet but under the rose there must be a body. Under the rose and under the mulch, its flesh is starting to sour. According to every *CSI* I've ever seen, after this length of time the body should be a good distance down the road to decomposition. Especially in this weather. My brain is telling me this and I'm trying to tell it that I don't want to fucking know. I'm trying not to think of that cracked porcelain doll's face. That cloud of frizzy red hair. I'm trying not to think of her skin putrefying and sliding off her bones. I'm trying not to think of her belly blowing up with gases until her insides liquefy and dribble out her own anus. I'm trying not to think of the smell. Of the flies.

Right now I hate Dr Thorpe more than anything.

I retch and I retch and I retch.

And now there's the sound of tyres on gravel.

I straighten up and me and Seán look at each other and we stand like pagan ogham stones. My mind is thinking there's no way that could be the doctor back. He couldn't have finished already. And then it's thinking, maybe he forgot something or there was a mix-up with the tee-offs. And then it's thinking *ohshitohshitohshitohshitohshit*.

From around the front of the house I can hear a car door slam.

Out of a black well of horror I can hear my voice go, 'Seán, we have to get the fuck out of here. We have to get the fuck out of here now.'

Seán says, 'But we haven't found her, yet.'

And then he goes, 'What if she isn't here?'

I can hear the doubt in him. It's like something lost in the dark.

I look from Seán to the hole between my feet and back again. I'm standing there like a moron and, like I have no control over it any more, I hear my voice go, 'She's here. She's right here. I can smell her.'

Seán looks from the house to me and then back to the house again and he goes, 'We may run. I don't want to get into any more trouble.'

We can't be found here. I know this with all the certainty that I know I saw what I saw. I'm looking at Seán and I'm looking at the back wall and then I get an idea. I'm swallowing what feels like a knot of oily rags in my gullet and I'm going, 'We'll run around the front. Dr Thorpe's inside the house. If he goes into the kitchen, he'll see us. If we head out the front at least he might be afraid of other people seeing him.'

And just like that me and Seán are turning to run.

We tear around the front of the house and any second I'm expecting to hear Dr Thorpe's voice yelling at us. We pound around the corner and there's Dr Thorpe's car. In the sunlight it looks like a giant, carapaced insect. It is still running and the front door to Dr Thorpe's house is standing open and I can imagine the fake pine smell curling out from it. At the bottom of the drive the black iron gates are open too. Me and Seán don't even have to say anything, we just barrel straight down the drive toward those gates and away from the horror of Dr Thorpe's house.

Me and Seán run and run and we're near the gates when a shout comes from behind us.

'Hey, stop! What the fuck were you at?'

And then Dr Thorpe's voice takes on a ragged edge and his next words sound sort of splintered like the scream of a seagull. He screams, 'You little fuckers! What were you doing in my house? Get the back here!'

I'm thinking he obviously hasn't seen the garden yet. I'm thinking that when he does he's going to come after us.

We, me and Seán, are through the gates now and we're on the Nunnery Road. We pitch right and centrifugal force hurls me out on to the road before I yaw back onto the path. Me and Seán are running harder than I ever thought it possible for someone to run. I am borne on a jet of pure adrenaline. Terror propels me forward. Terror carries me toward the barricades a hundred yards in front of us.

Beside me Seán's heavy head is a dull ball of concentration but I'm giggling as I run. With an awful clarity I realise that I'm on the verge of hysteria.

In front of us the orange plastic barriers are manned by two guards who are paying absolutely no attention to us as we close the distance.

Then, without any warning, from behind us comes the bellow of a big diesel engine and Dr Thorpe's 407 slews out of his gate and onto the tarmac.

Seán looks behind him and goes, 'I'm scared.' Every syllable is punctuated by a whooping breath.

My voice is all high-pitched and warbling but I look at him and I say, 'Me too.'

The guards at the barricades are taking notice because two teenagers are sprinting towards them, closely followed by a gleaming black car that's rapidly gaining and you can hear the whine of the engine as it's pushed into the red before every gear shift.

We reach the barrier with about twenty yards to spare and behind us the sound of braking fills the world. The two guards step out from behind their barrier and one of them is saying something into his radio. The other one is transferring his gaze from us to Dr Thorpe's 407 and back to us again. Me and Seán try to get past them but the second one stops us and says, 'What's the problem lads?'

Before Seán can say anything, I go, 'There's no problem, Guard. We're just late meeting our friends in the Square.'

His buddy has by now strolled over to Dr Thorpe's car which has come to a stop up on the kerb much closer to us than I'd like. The guard is leaning in the passenger window and he's saying something to Dr Thorpe. Then he's straightening and then he's looking at us and then he beckons his partner over.

The guard says, 'Stay here.' And he walks over to where his buddy is talking with the good doctor.

Seán, standing beside me, goes, 'We're not staying here, are we?'

I look at him and then I look at the two guards and their cosy little chat with Dr Thorpe and I go, 'Stay here? No fucking way.'

Just as the second guard goes to turn away from the 407, me and Seán turn tail and run as hard as we can. I take a look over my shoulder and I can see the first guard saying something into his radio and I can see Dr Thorpe getting out of his car. His face is all hard and shiny and now instead of looking like Pat Kenny he looks like Henry Fonda at the start of *Once Upon a Time in the West*. And I'm thinking how blue blue his eyes are. And then I'm thinking of Henry Fonda again and then I'm thinking, *ohshitohshitohshitohshitohshit*.

During the Strawberry Fair there's only one place to go where you're going to be guaranteed a crowd so when we get to the Pig Market Hill we turn left down towards the Maket Square. Behind us the two guards and Dr Thorpe are sort of half jogging, half walking. They're doing this so that they don't attract too much attention. Because they're doing this though we're extending our lead on them.

We're about halfway down Main Street and the music from the makeshift stage down in the Square comes skirling up through the warm air. There are people here. Lots of people and the crowds are getting denser the further into town we get. Locals and tourists and families from out the country, all with tubs of strawberries in their fists and smears of cream slathered across their faces. Purple and gold shirts are everywhere. They don't notice anything except their own company and me and Seán hurry between them and behind us the two guards and Dr Thorpe are all spiky and urgent in their movements.

Me and Seán have stopped running now because once you get to the junction between Main Street and the Square you can't run anymore. It's too packed. Dr Thorpe is still behind us but now there's no sign of the two guards.

Out of breath, Seán goes, 'Where are we going?'

And exhausted I say, 'I don't know.'

There's something in Seán's face that makes me frown and I'm saying, 'What's wrong?'

Seán blinks real slowly and his big shoulders shift uncomfortably and he goes, 'Are you sure you saw what you saw? We're going to get in loads of trouble if you didn't see anything.'

In the middle of this crowd of people I go, 'For fuck's sake, Seán. Not you too?'

Seán blinks again, real slow, and now I'm worried because he doesn't say anything. He just looks at me with his great sad eyes.

Still frowning, I go, 'Come on.'

We're wending our way through the crowds but it's impossible to see where we're going and I'm just waiting for a guard's big hand to land on my shoulder or Dr Thorpe to head us off. Ten or fifteen yards behind us I can hear him apologising to people for barging into them.

Up on the bandstand a rubber chicken outfit of two guitarists and a drum machine are playing 'Kelly the Boy from Killann'. The crowd are loving it.

In front of us one of the guards from the barrier pushes through the crowd like an ice-breaker. His eyes are looking ahead at something and his gaze slides right over our heads but I can feel my bladder spasm anyway. Me and Seán stop talking and he passes within a few yards of us as the gold sun of freedom darkens at Ross.

We duck down as low as we can without attracting attention. I'm peeking out through a meaty fence of arms and hips and torsos and I'm terrified but I'm trying to think of what to do. I'm trying to think of some way to get away from here. Around the square there's a ring of guards and if they're all pals with Dr Thorpe then we're well and truly fucked. Even if they're not we have no way of knowing until it's too late. I'm thinking, if only there was a way of letting everyone know all at once. *Everyone* couldn't be in on it.

And on the bandstand the lead singer is braying out that dauntless Kelly is Mount Leinster's own darling and pride and then I'm turning to Seán and I'm going, 'Come on.'

I'm looking at the bandstand and then I'm grabbing Seán by the collar and I'm going, 'Just follow me.'

We're pushing through the crowd and I'm going, 'Excuse me. Sorry. Coming through.' There's people getting annoyed and there's this ripple of disgruntlement spreading out from where we're moving.

Off to the right I catch a glimpse of Dr Thorpe and I know

that he sees me because he starts angling toward us. He's moving through the crowd a lot more elegantly now that he can see us. Under his petrified quiff, his face is hot and slick with sweat.

Right in front of the stage the festival organisers have placed the white plastic lawn furniture. This tacky seating area is lightly populated with a scattering of old men and women who sit there with their handbags on their laps and their walking sticks on the ground and expressions of contentment on their faces. Me and Seán barrel through them towards the stage. Brilliantly, one old man with skin like yellow paper and liver spots all over his bald skull lets out a roar on our way by and swings his stick at us.

Seán is moaning now and because we're clattering through the plastic seating, the crowd no longer hides us. Out in the open like this we are the focus of every eye in the Square. The thing is Dr Thorpe can see this too and he's stopped on the edge of the crowd like a swimmer afraid to get in the pool. His face is this weird shade of red that I've never seen before. It's like his veins and cap-illaries are flushing madder beneath his skin.

Everyone is looking at us and even the band have stopped playing.

Everyone is looking at us as me and Seán vault over the waist-high steel fence that protects the stage. Everyone is looking at us as me and Seán climb up onto the stage and look out over the crowd. Every face is turned towards us and every eye sees us standing there and down in the crowd I can see Dr Thorpe take a step forward.

Behind us the lead singer of the band goes, 'Lads, we're trying to play a gig here. Would ye stop the messing.'

Seán turns around to face him and there must be something desperate in the way he looks right now because the man shuts up and he and his mates back away from us and keep right on backing away.

Out in front, Dr Thorpe takes another hesistant step toward the stage and before I know what I'm doing I'm lifting my arms up and I'm shouting out over the crowd, 'Everyone! You have to listen to me!'

There's a bleating note to my words and people are pointing fingers and laughing and through the crowd there's a few guards starting to push their way to us. People aren't paying any attention to what I'm trying to say and I'm starting to get frantic. There must be a few lads from school in the crowd as well because slowly at first but gathering tempo and volume a chant is building.

Woof. Woof. Woof. Woof.

Out of the big field of faces in front of me the chant gets louder.

Woof. Woof. Woof. Woof.

Dr Thorpe takes another step. And another. And another.

Then there's the squeal of feedback and I'm swinging the abandoned microphone in front of my face. All of a sudden I can hear my own breathing coming from the monitors at the front of the stage. It sounds like a sea in storm.

Because I'm an idiot I go, 'Um . . .'

And out over the crowd my idiocy carries, amplified and distorted and humming with static.

Ummmmmm . . . .

I can't hear the chant now. All I can hear is my own breathing and the rush of my own pulse in my ears.

Through the mic and out over the crowd I go, 'Everyone! You have to listen!'

I'm standing too close to the mic and the feedback makes everyone wince but I keep going. I'm saying, 'You have to listen to me.'

Below me Dr Thorpe has almost reached the metal fencing in front of the bandstand. I'm pointing at him and I'm going, 'That man is a murderer!'

As these words come out of my mouth, Dr Thorpe stops and his eyes lift to meet mine and his face is crawling with fury. I'm standing like a preacher on a mount with my outstretched left hand pointing at him and it's like I've transfixed him where he stands.

The whole crowd goes quiet. In the wake of the fading feedback comes an electric hush. Even the *woofs* have all died away. Not a word is spoken and everyone is looking at Dr Thorpe and frowns are starting to crease people's faces. Out in the mass of people the guards stop too and in the silence I can hear the crackle of one of their radios.

Dr Thorpe stares up at me and all of a sudden I'm reminded of Seán. There's broken glass in that look. There are blades in it.

All the while Seán is moaning to himself. Under his breath

but loud in the silence I can hear Seán going, 'We're in so much trouble. We're in so much trouble.'

The crowd is starting to bubble again now and there's an edge to people's voices. This time it's not derision. This time there are no mocking chants. Just a saw blade of anger blended with a lot of confusion. The crowd is on the verge of becoming a mob.

And all the while, Seán's going, 'We're in so much trouble. We're in so much trouble.'

Seán is looking at me now and across his face all the muscles are squirming like there's something vile under his skin. His eyes are looking at me and in them I can see all the hurt he's ever felt. Every jeer and every sneer stares back out at me and now Seán's going, 'I don't want to be a freak anymore.'

'I don't want to be a freak anymore.'

Over and over he says this and every time he says it his voice gets just a little louder. Without his meds Seán's pretty fucked up. And now I'm starting to worry about him. About us.

Looking at Dr Thorpe with his talk-show host's hair and his middle starting to slacken you wouldn't think he'd have it in him. You wouldn't think he'd be able to clear the metal fence and vault so easily up onto the bandstand. You wouldn't think it. But he does.

Dr Thorpe is standing on the bandstand beside me and Seán and he starts moving towards us. He walks like the Terminator out of *Terminator 2*. Not the Arnie one but the other one. The one made out of liquid metal. He moves like he's fluid but cutting all at once. His features are smouldering.

I'm leaning into the mic and the static is whip-cracking again and over Seán's mounting volume I'm practically yelling stuff. Down in the crowd people's faces are starting to crumple at the noise and everyone looks like they've swallowed something really sour.

I'm pointing and going, 'That man, there. Dr Thorpe. You have to do something. I saw him. I really saw him.'

Dr Thorpe's face is all twisted and anxious and there's terror as well as anger crawling in him. Dr Thorpe is looking at me and Seán and it's like he suddenly realises where he is. He swallows hard and you can here the little glug of his bobbing Adam's Apple. He looks at us and in this weird plaintive voice he goes, 'What were you doing at my house? What have I ever done to you?'

And then Seán is beside me and his big hands are bunching around the base of the mic. This close to my eyes I can see the wrinkles of his thick fingers all corrugated and silted with grime. His nails are all broken from where he picks at them. I know this. He doesn't bite them. He curls one hand into the other and he picks at them. Around his nails the skin is all callused and cracked.

These fingers, my best friend's thick, ragged fingers, they curl around the base of the mic and then they unplug the jack.

Just like that.

When the jack comes out of the plug there's a thump of noise like a detonation and when the speakers blow you can actually feel the concussion. You know in that movie *Das Boot*? It's like that. A depth-charge.

Then there's a silence. A world-filling silence. And into this silence, Seán, with his big hands still holding the mic and still holding the flaccid jack, goes, 'I don't want to be a freak anymore.'

When I look into his big face I see the same expression that people use to look at him. There's this sort of pity in his eyes and this sort of disgust and this sort of disbelief. And right now I know that Seán doesn't want to do this anymore. All the others with their *woofs* and their insults, all the others with their cruelty and disdain. All these people have beaten him. Anymore, he doesn't want to be different.

And up on this bandstand with people staring at us and Dr Thorpe's face a hanging mask of empty sacking I know that Seán has chosen them over me. Over us.

And just like that I can see in his face the questions that he's never ever asked before. Behind his cobbles for eyes for the first time ever he doubts me. I know that in his head his own version of Judas is bawling, *You never saw anything.* He's saying, *Dr Thorpe wouldn't do something like that.* He's saying, *Nobody can believe the Lord's prayer out of you.* Seán doesn't trust me.

And Judas laughs and laughs and laughs.

And my anger rises measure for measure.

There's a display table on the bandstand stacked high with local produce for all to see. Juices, jams, chutneys. The works. My swinging fist connects with the side of Seán's face and he flounders into it. Seán doesn't deserve this. I know straightaway that he doesn't but his nose and lips pretty much disintegrate into a cloud of red. It reminds me of the dead girl's hair. Frothy and ephemeral.

His fall smashes half the display stuff to atoms.

His fall breaks something inside of me.

In the middle of a morass of chutney and glass Seán is on his back and he lies there blinking up at me and Dr Thorpe.

And just like that I'm left on my own and in my ears the sound of my fist connecting with Seán Galvin's flesh is horrible and familiar. The dead meat smack of it.

The red stuff that Seán's lying in definitely isn't blood. It's too red red. It's not warm enough and it's not dark enough and it's not like the stuff coming from his nose.

For Seán, the world must rock to the concussion of being blind-sided.

This is the day I lose the best part of my life. Today I've lost the best part of my life.

This is the day, with the sun rabies-hot in the sky and every face in the Market Square hanging open. Every mouth is a shocked black hole and I don't know what I'm screaming but I'm screaming something.

Jam. Seán is lying in strawberry jam.

I'm looking at him and hate myself for what I just did. My hand is aching already from where it connected with Seán's face. I'm pretty sure that I'm going to have flecks of Seán's skin smeared across my knuckles.

Down below, the crowd is evaporating except for a load of guards who are trying to fight through the streams of people to reach the stage. Even over the screams you can hear the robot voices coming from their radios. These bodiless voices sound panicked. It's like the guy up in the barracks operating the dispatch is having a fit. I can imagine him yammering into his headset as every light on his control board comes on all at once and starts winking at him.

Down in the Square, I can see Guard Devlin. He's just standing there but I can remember the way he looked at me in Dr Thorpe's house. The way he grinned like a Great White with his big, fat, wide head, all muscle and snaggle-teeth. I remember it like it's happening again in front of me. Guard Devlin stands there and ignores everything. He ignores the scattering crowd. He ignores the other guards moving confused and tense amongst the upended lawn furniture. He ignores Dr Thorpe standing baffled and frantic beside Seán. Seán is moaning again. He ignores all this and he just stares at me for a minute with my breath coming in gasps between my screams and my eyes wide and my hands clenching and unclenching.

And now I can hear what I'm screaming. I'm screaming, 'You have to believe us. We're not freaks. We're really not freaks!'

Beside me Seán is moaning and from his nose and lips the blood just spreads and spreads and spreads.

I get this leaflet to explain why I'm here. This is what the opening paragraph says: *If you are suffering from a mental disorder, you may go into a psychiatric hospital or unit voluntarily, or you may be committed as an involuntary patient. The vast majority of admissions are voluntary – this means that you freely agree to go for treatment. Voluntary psychiatric patients are not completely free to leave psychiatric care and may be detained for a period and may then be involuntarily detained. There are detailed rules about the detention of patients involuntarily.*

They won't even talk about letting me out of here yet so I presume I'm not one of *the vast majority.*

Nobody believes me and nobody listens to me. I keep trying to tell people that I'm grand. That I'm not fucked up. People smile and nod and take notes on clipboards and then leave again.

Seán visits sometimes. He is back on his meds now and he seems to be doing well. He says Mr Cowper was asking for me.

The irony of all this is lost on him.